Emma Jeanne and Ralph

A DRAMATIC TALE ABOUT AFRICAN AMERICAN FOLKLORE IN THE OLD SOUTH

MAURICE HAMILTON

HAYMAKER PUBLISHING
CHARLOTTE, NORTH CAROLINA

EMMA JEANNE AND RALPH

A DRAMATIC TALE ABOUT
AFRICAN AMERICAN FOLKLORE
IN THE OLD SOUTH

© Copyright 2017
By Maurice Hamilton
Charlotte, NC

Library of Congress Control Number: 2017942566
International Standard Book Number: 978-0-9839278-8-4

Acknowledgements and Dedications

*First, I want to thank God for allowing me to be used as a
vessel to speak to all those who read this book.
Thank you Heavenly Father.*

*This book is dedicated to my family and friends who have given me
their love, counsel and support even during times of doubts.*

*Very special and heartfelt thank you to the editors at Scribendi who
helped me put this story in literary form.*

CONTENTS

PREFACE

Emma Jeanne and Ralph is a book that was been inspired by my own recollections, events, and perspectives from my life experience as a young boy living in the South. While reading it, please keep in mind that it is a novella.

INTRODUCTION
THE HISTORY OF HAMMONDSVILLE

During the early 1950s the town of Hammondsville, South Carolina, was occupied mostly by black people. It was a farming town with a population of approximately two thousand people, 65 percent black and 35 percent white. Blacks and whites living there found ways to work together even though segregation was visible and practiced daily.

Blacks there were hard-working, patriotic people who made measurable progress in spite of being denied their rights to be free human beings in the place where they were born. The nine-mile-square town was founded in 1853 by a white man named Steve Hammonds. Under his ownership it became the Hammonds Plantation. Steve and his wife, Vera Mae, owned over 250 slaves who worked twelve-hour days to make sure the plantation survived and remained prosperous. The Hammonds hired some poor whites to help with the farming and oversee the slaves.

Steve would sometimes direct his white overseers to randomly select a slave and beat him for no reason except to keep them in line.

They both wanted children very badly, but they suffered one tragedy after the next when it came to procreation. They had five pregnancies in total, but Vera miscarried twice during her first pregnancies. They waited awhile and tried again. This time they were sure they were going to have a child. Vera Mae went full term, but this little baby boy, Steve Jr., died after only two months. They waited a little longer before trying again. Things were looking great this time. Vera Mae went through a full term and had twin boys, Jonathan and Joshua. They were born with Dravet syndrome, a severe form of epilepsy. They were always sick, and both of them died before their fifth birthday.

Being unable to have children hurt both Steve and Vera. Steve's family was also experiencing one tragic death after the next. His only brother, James (Jimmy), and one sister, Alice, were already dead. He and his sister, Sally Mae, were the only living family members left. Although Steve was considered a very strong man, the painful ritual of expecting a child only to watch the child die took its toll. Vera watched him wallow in his pain and cry out, "Why? Oh my Lord, why can't my wife give me healthy children?" Vera sat next to him one of those nights and told him what she thought the reason was. She told him they were cursed because of the misery they caused in the lives of their slaves. She really resented him having sex with the slave women and the next night wanting to have sex with her.

There were many times when Steve would have a few drinks, go into the slave quarters, and beat a male slave for no apparent reason. He also raped several of his female slaves during his drunken escapades. After all, they were his property because he'd bought them. He owned everything on his land. He could do whatever he wanted to do with his property. He had sex with them whenever he felt the need. As much as Vera hated his behavior, she didn't argue with him about it because when she did he made her feel guilty by reminding her that she couldn't bear him any children. It was rumored all around the plantation that Steve had fathered several children by his female slaves.

There was an undeniable resemblance between Steve and a number of his slaves, but this one young male slave, Amos Hammonds, was the spitting image of Steve. He had very fair skin and red, curly hair, just like Steve. Steve decided to make sure this boy got special treatment. Vera was a teacher before marriage, and Steve made her teach Amos to read and write. From that point on, his biological mother was no longer a part of his life. He was taken from her and there was nothing she could do about it.

Amos was gifted with natural intelligence and Vera did such a good job that when the tall, slender Amos turned eighteen, he was fully prepared for a university-level education. The Hammonds sent him to Baldwin University in New York. Six years later he received a Ph.D. in Agricultural Science. Steve, Vera, and Sally Mae attended the graduation ceremony. They were all proud of Amos and treated him as though he was the white son Steve and Vera had always wanted. His biological mother did not attend her son's graduation nor was she aware he was graduating.

Steve allowed Amos to move into their big antebellum style house and Vera treated him like he was her own son. He spent the next five years at the plantation, getting hands-on experience in how to operate his father's business. In 1882 Steve died from a massive heart attack. Before he died he made Amos promise he'd take care of Vera and Sally Mae. They were both getting up in age and were in very poor health. A few months before his death, Steve had felt the need to make restitution to his remaining slaves, whom he had brutally abused over the years. He gave each family a plot of land and allowed them to build their own home on their land.

He signed the plantation over to Amos and acknowledged him as his biological son. There were many white people in that county who vehemently opposed that decision. They tried to threaten and bully Amos and take the plantation from him. Amos managed to successfully ward them off with the help of many of his dad's white friends. Some of these white men were powerful politicians in the county and in Washington, D.C. Through all the difficulties, Amos managed to keep the farm and do business with whites, who were often skeptical at first. Many of them still weren't sure they should do business with this mulatto man who looked more white than black.

The Ku Klux Klan (KKK) was especially troublesome. They would often try to intimidate Amos by coming onto the plantation to burn crosses, fire their guns, or threaten Amos and his wife and children. He was determined to keep his plantation and would not let those threats deter him. He eventually dropped the word "plantation" and renamed the small Southern town Hammondsville, South Carolina. Most of the men who came were veterans of the Civil War. Some of them were Union Soldiers who got stuck in the South and decided to make Hammondsville their home, as well.

By 1890 many more black people made Hammondsville their home because it was a place where they could own property and live as free people. The freedom black people experienced, was due to Amos' ability to connect with some top political figures that were still loyal to Steve.

Oil was discovered in Hammondsville in 1921 and Amos gave 68% of the profits to The Capital Oil Company.

They were an experienced company that came in and built the oil well, refined the oil, and brought it to the market. Oil was in great demand, so 32% was enough revenue to support the needs of the city as well as yield a profit to its black and white shareholders.

Some white owned banks operating under Jim Crow laws took many properties from blacks. Amos Hammonds, Jr.'s Solvent Savings Bank was the first black owned and operated black in that part of the South. There was a branch in each town. These banks held mortgages on most homes and they went out of their way to help families save their homes and their land. They also felt comfortable depositing their money in that bank. White banks would sometimes keep their money. This led to many black people hiding their money under mattresses or burying it in tin cans.

Allied Trading Company was a black owned and operated shipping company that pitched in its fair share of revenue towards the three black towns. They shipped goods on their 275 ton ship (Ya Meli) locally from their dock in Puerto Grande, S.C. to a port in Helsingborg, Sweden. Black farmers sold lots of fresh produce as well. A large percentage of the profits earned were used to build and maintain the schools, roads, and municipal properties in Hammondsville, Bridgeport, and Gifford.

During the 1920s both blacks and whites held political offices in these towns. White people were in the minority, yet they still controlled much of the government in those cities. However, many of them began sharing political tickets with blacks to make sure they get elected to office. On many occasions, laws passed to protect blacks were violated by whites. Many white people gave blacks enough support to keep their towns a great place to reside and raise a family. Those white people were longtime residents and felt like they had an investment in the city's survival. They pooled their money so that very little of it was wasted.

During the next half century, the town of Hammondsville survived many racial skirmishes that sometimes turned into hard-fought wars. There were innumerable organized and unprovoked physical attacks on innocent black people by groups of white men in public places all across this town, as there were throughout the South. Black people always manage to survive, regroup, and rebuild their lives.

Fighting off the Klan wasn't the only threat to their existence. They often experienced very bad weather. Hammondsville is a coastal town located between Orchard Beach and Puerto Grande, and like all the towns near the ocean, it experiences thunderstorms and hurricanes as well. The people of Hammondsville not only survived, but there were times they flourished after storms.

People who made Hammondsville their home loved living there. They were determined to accept the many challenges that came their way. Both blacks and whites worked together to rebuild the town and make many improvements. Each time tragedy struck and it looked like Hammondsville was weakening, the people came together and did what it took to bring it back and made it stronger than ever before. It was when they built a sewer system and installed indoor plumbing in most houses that angered many white people in nearby towns. They didn't like seeing blacks living as well as they did.

As the years passed, more whites moved into Hammondsville and even though they had a smaller population they controlled most of the town's government. Blacks living there were in a continuous struggle to change the "Jim Crow Laws" so they could enjoy their freedom as first class American citizens.

As late as 1953, "Jim Crow" still maintained a chokehold on the civil and human rights of black people. Codes of conduct for blacks were still strictly enforced in most towns. Black citizens living in Hammondsville weren't treated quite as bad. This was partly due to the fact that it was populated by more blacks than whites and blacks there had gained some political power. However, there were separate public facilities, such as hotels, bathrooms, and schools. They were strictly separated by the concept of de jure segregation or segregation of black and white people by law. Blacks still had to sit in the back of the bus and go to the back of restaurants to get take-out food. Interracial marriage was illegal. In fact, a black male could lose his life by just looking at a white female.

Many black people owned their homes in Hammondsville, but some whites frowned on that idea. They didn't believe blacks should own anything, especially land and property. Secondly, they had an image of black people as lazy and stupid, but blacks in Hammondsville proved them wrong. These black men and women were hard-working homeowners and business owners. They were achieving success in spite of the Jim Crow restrictions. The black church played a major role in setting the moral compass for black people. However, the strict code of behavior was very difficult to abide by. As the story unfolds we shall see that these codes were no match for the raging teenage hormones.

CHAPTER 1
EMMA JEANNE AND RALPH

Emma Jeanne Jones and Ralph Cunningham are both eighteen years old. They met at an annual baseball game at Hammondsville High School. Ralph was the star player on the visiting team. He was a tall, lean, physically fit young man who loved playing baseball. Just six years earlier, Jackie Robinson had broken Major League Baseball's color barrier when the Brooklyn Dodgers started him at first base. Robinson immediately became Ralph's hero, and baseball was the game that was going to make him a star. He was a rising star during his senior year at Fredrick Douglas High School. His team, the Skyhawks, was proud to have him as their captain. The high school was located in Bridgeport, about eight miles northwest of Hammondsville.

Ralph's athletic ability was recognized early by the school's baseball coach, and he decided to teach him everything he knew about the game. Baseball became Ralph's first love, so much so that he hardly thought about anything else. However, there were times that all that attention to baseball interfered with his schoolwork. He had to be disciplined a couple of times because his grades in some of his classes dropped from an A to a C. There was no doubt that he was capable of mastering the classwork, and If he needed help there were many family members who were capable tutors in most school subjects. He just had to learn to balance the time he spent on his schoolwork and the time he spent on baseball practice. He needed to allocate equal time to both. His love of baseball also hurt his relationship with his girlfriend, Hazel Williams. She ended their two-year relationship because she felt that he gave too much attention to baseball and not enough to her.

One day when he came to visit her, she told him "We're finished Mr. Ralph Cunningham! I will not play second to your baseball. It's obvious that you care more about that than me." "What's wrong?" Ralph asked. "What's right with this relationship Ralph? I haven't seen or heard from you in two weeks. I don't need this kind of a relationship. There are too many fish in the sea." Then, she slammed the door in his face. Ralph was looking at the ground as he walked away thinking to himself, "I'll find another girlfriend."

On July 4, 1953, the town of Hammondsville was preparing to have their annual amateur all-star baseball game. On Independence Day, all-star games were played throughout the country. This particular game was special because Hammondsville and Gifford were predominantly black towns with some of the best amateur baseball players in the country. This was also an important game because college baseball recruiters were going to attend, scouting the most talented players and offering them full scholarships. The high stakes made Ralph a little nervous, but he was prepared to show all his skills. His team, the Skyhawks, was the visiting team. They were a very competitive, all-black high school team. The hometown team, the Bulldogs, knew they had their work cut out for them. They had played games against the Skyhawk's before and lost.

People from all areas of the South and from as far North as Virginia, attended this major event. It was the largest crowd to date. The game was a little slow getting the crowd excited, but at the bottom of the third inning Ralph hit a home run. It was another of his shining moments, and the excitement of the huge crowd of baseball fans exploded. Now the Skyhawk's were up 2–0.

In the fifth inning there was more excitement. Ralph was up to bat again. He hit the first pitch hard, sending it towards the head of the third baseman. As he tried catching the ball, it hit the side of his glove and rolled around on the ground. By the time he got the ball and threw it, Ralph was at home plate. The catcher there was blocking the plate. Ralph tried to slide under the catcher, but he didn't quite touch the base before being tagged out. The umpire saw it and yelled, "You're out!"

Ralph became so angry at the catcher for blocking the plate that he said to him "You little bitch." Then he stood there giving him an angry stare. His teammates quickly subdued Ralph and took him off the field before things got any worse. He was benched for the rest of the game. The Skyhawks won the game with a final score of 3–2. Ralph was sitting in the dugout feeling bad that he couldn't control his temper. He realized that by losing his cool he had also lost what might have been his only opportunity to get a college scholarship.

Emma Jeanne attended this game with her girlfriend Mary Parker. She didn't know Ralph personally, but she had seen him play baseball against her school and against another high school in Gifford earlier that spring. She had become one of Ralph's many fans. When she saw how he reacted after he was tagged out, she felt sorry for him. She knew what this game meant to the players and what was at stake. So she decided she would introduce herself and offer some words of encouragement.

Emma Jeanne walked over to Ralph and said, "Hey, Ralph, you play a great game of baseball."

"Thanks," Ralph said, looking down in shame for his bad behavior.

She told him, "I was a little surprised at your reaction for being tagged out."

He told her, "There was a lot at stake, and I got angry and frustrated. I am sorry, but I couldn't help it at that moment. I felt like the catcher was in the way of my career goal."

"Yeah, but you only made things worse," she responded.

Ralph agreed and started to feel better now that he'd talked to someone who seemed to understand. He finally looked up and stared at her as she spoke to him. Emma Jeanne was a stunningly beautiful young woman, and Ralph wondered why he'd never paid attention to her. He couldn't say much to her because her best friend, Mary, was there with her, listening to his every word and staring at him from head to toe. He did manage to tell Emma Jeanne that he would be at the school dance later that evening. He whispered to her, "Come alone." She told him she couldn't come alone, but she'd be there.

Emma Jeanne knew her parents, Fred and Henrietta, wouldn't allow her to go to the school dance alone. She and Mary went to the party together and met up with Ralph. He came with his best friend and teammate, Benny Lee Williams. They were all young adults and their hormones were running wild.

They went inside the large school cafeteria and danced for about fifteen minutes. Then, Ralph and Emma Jeanne decided to leave Mary and Benny Lee.

Emma Jeanne told them, "I am going to show Ralph around, and we'll meet back here later."

Mary and Benny Lee agreed, but Mary asked, "What time are you coming back?"

"In about an hour," Emma Jeanne responded, smiling as she walked away with Ralph. "Wow, you're gonna miss the whole dance." Mary told her. "No I won't." Said Emma Jeanne while walking away laughing.

Emma Jeanne really admired Ralph, and she kind of put him on a pedestal. She wanted to have a nice conversation to let him know that she liked him. She said to him, "Boy, I really enjoyed that game today."

"Yeah, it was okay," Ralph said while looking down at the ground, still feeling ashamed about his behavior.

"What happened today is past and you should try to get past it. Remember, you're still a big-time hero around here," Emma Jeanne said with a big, beautiful smile.

Ralph looked at her and said, "You think so?"

"Yes, I know so," Emma Jeanne responded.

They finally found a spot where they could be alone. It was the maintenance building behind the school. It was unlocked, so they went inside and closed the door behind them. Ralph pulled out his little whisky flask and offered Emma Jeanne a drink. She looked almost ashamed to admit it, but she said, "I never drank liquor before."

"Just taste a little bit," Ralph said. "It won't hurt you. You'll like it."

Emma Jeanne was still hesitant to take that drink.

"Do you want me to go first?" Ralph asked.

"Yeah, you go first."

Ralph took a big gulp and handed it to her, saying, "See that didn't hurt."

Emma Jeanne grabbed the flask from him and took a little swig.

Ralph took his flask back and said, "You've got to do better than that." He took another big gulp and handed it back to her.

By now, Emma Jeanne was caught up in the excitement of proving she could do something she had never done before. She took a big gulp like Ralph.

"Wow!" Ralph said with excitement in his voice. "Now that's what I'm talking about."

Emma Jeanne was starting to feel a little tipsy from the alcohol and beginning to lower her inhibitions. Ralph could see that she was quickly dropping her guard. He seized the moment, grabbed her, and French kissed her. She felt bold and responded with the same passion. Things continued to heat up between them until all of a sudden, she said, "Stop, Ralph."

"Oh my God, what's wrong?" He asked.

"I think we're moving too fast."

"No we're not. I want you badly. I can feel you want me too," he said while attempting to kiss her again. "Come on, it's okay," Ralph promised.

Emma Jeanne was feeling sexy and confused at the same time. Her mind was in seesaw mode. One minute it was *yes, go ahead*, and the next minute it was *no, don't do it*. Finally, she gave in to Ralph's demands.

Ralph could sense that this was her first time, so he tried to be gentle with her. He didn't want her to tell him to stop again. They finally got into a groove and she began experiencing feelings that she'd never felt before. It was a great feeling of ecstasy!

They went back to meet up with Mary and Benny Lee, acting like nothing had happened. After returning home, Emma Jeanne went straight to her room and fell asleep. While taking a bath for church the next morning, she saw some blood on her pubic hairs. There was no pain, so she finished her bath. She had been a virgin and knew that a little bleeding could result. She got dressed and went to church with her family. She was feeling ashamed and guilty. She felt like she had violated all the moral principles she was taught.

"My God," she thought. "If only I could relive last night. I would not have gone all the way with Ralph." The feelings of guilt haunted her.

As the church services progressed, Rev. Fitzgerald stepped up to the pulpit and announced that the sermon would be about "Guilt and Shame." Emma Jeanne was in touch with her feelings, and she knew she was feeling a lot of guilt because of what she had done the night before. For a second, she wondered if Rev. Fitzgerald knew what she'd done and was going to talk about it in front of everybody. She asked herself, "Oh my God, does everybody know what I did?"

Rev. Fitzgerald began his sermon by stating: "Guilt and shame seem to be identical, but they're not. Guilt is about an act that we commit that goes against our moral teachings. If we don't forgive ourselves and ask God to forgive us, the guilt will turn into shame. Shame is who we become as a result of our guilt. It will stay on your mind and torture you."

Emma Jeanne felt like Rev. Fitzgerald was reading her mind. He went on to say: "Some people try to get instant relief from the torture by using drugs, alcohol, comfort foods, and sex. As Christians we learn to turn to God and ask him to take these painful feelings of guilt and shame away. We cannot remove the guilt and shame ourselves. Self cannot save self. We need a savior. God is our only savior. So, my church family, when you feel guilt and shame, turn to God and seek his help to deal with this affliction. You can't do it yourself, but God can, and he will if you simply ask him."

CHAPTER 2
EMMA JEANNE'S UPBRINGING

The lives of Emma Jeanne and her siblings, Fred Jr. and Thelma Mae, were consumed with church and school. That's where they learned to play the piano and sing in the choir. Fred Jr. also played the electric guitar. They got their moral compass from their parents and the church. This is where they learned the Ten Commandments and about God and the New Testament of the Bible. In school, they learned the Golden Rule, how to read, write, and do math. That's also where they learned how to study and what it meant to persevere. There were several sports programs at school, including track and field, basketball, baseball, and football. So learning about good sportsmanship and how to lose gracefully was very important.

Emma Jeanne and her siblings were rarely bored. They went skating and bowling on weekends. They also participated in school plays. They had a record player and played lots of rock 'n' roll, and blues songs they bought with their earnings from working part-time. They all had chores to do inside and outside the house. Overall, they lived innocent lives. They got into an occasional fight with classmates, but the school had in place a conflict resolution program. This program was designed to teach students alternative ways to solve emotional disputes that involved anger. They were taught to look at how the problem got started and the role they had played in creating it in the first place. Anyone who got into fights while at school had to attend those classes. This program significantly reduced physical fighting in and out of school.

Emma Jeanne was a smart, college-bound student. She wanted to be a teacher. As the eldest of the three children in her family, she was expected to set a good example. They were all two years apart. Except for the occasional invasion by white racists, Hammondsville was an ideal place for blacks to live and raise a family. There were lots of things to do. There were three churches in town with three different religious denominations. The largest congregation was at Mt. Shiloh Baptist. The next in size was the African Methodist Episcopal Zion Church, and then the Emanuel Pentecostal Church.

Each of these churches had very active youth programs, including basketball, youth choirs, bands, Bible studies, and summer youth programs. Grown folks had lots of things to do as well. In town, there was also a bowling alley, a skating rink, restaurants, and three nightspots.

Emma Jeanne became pregnant as a result of her one night stand with Ralph. She regretted making the decision to have sex with him. Although she'd been taught not to harbor anger and resentments, there were times she had a very strong resentment towards Ralph and her family. She didn't' realize how much trouble she would cause her family and herself by dropping her guards just one night. It was not only her reputation on the line, but her parents came under scrutiny as well. People at church wondered if her parents were too liberal with her. This angered her parents because they thought they had raised a good girl who would grow up, get married and have children like they did. During her pregnancy, her mother would say, "You're the first born child and you are supposed to set the example for you brother and sister."

Although most of the church family was very supportive and understood that these things happens with young adults. Many of them had that experience themselves. They were just lucky there was it didn't result in a pregnancy. Even with that support, going to church was not the same for Emma Jeanne and her family, they felt shame and guilt for a while.

The church played a major role in setting the moral compass for the community. In situations like these, the church got involved because they wanted to help the family during this difficult time. They were also concerned that Emma Jean would have multiple children by multiple men and still not be married. When that happened to a woman, she was considered loose or unable to control her sex life. Some people even caller that type of woman a whore or a nymphomaniac. So, women really had to be extra careful about their sexual activity because one mistake could cost them their reputation.

It didn't apply equally for men. In some circles, a man may be complimented for being a stud. According to Rev. Fitzgerald, this may have been one of those evil remnants from slavery. He explained that back then, the white man owned everything he bought, including the black people. So, the more babies the young buck made, the more slaves he had to sell or use as field hands to work his plantation.

Another concern the church had with having sex outside of marriage could result in being exposed to diseases. They believed that, more sex partners a person had the more likely they could get a sexually transmitted disease. At that time, a women's body was considered a vessel of virtue. Remember, we are in the south and a woman's body was like a field that would accept the seed of life. If this field was unhealthy, then, anything that grows from it will be affected. Human life came through her body; therefore, it was her responsibility to maintain a disease free, healthy body. The church and Emma Jeanne's parents knew all these things, but somehow they forgot to discuss them with her. Back then, people didn't talk about sex with their children. In church, they gave the impression that people didn't have sex, but members all knew all those babies came from somewhere.

Emma Jeanne's parents began watching her closer than ever before. Emma Jeanne wondered why they didn't give her all this parental advice before she became pregnant. She was beginning to feel like having this baby was a big mistake that will never go away. Her mother, reminded her of her error in judgment too often. It created a break in their mother/ daughter bond. Her dad told her that he still loved her, but he was disappointed in her. Emma Jeanne wished that she could turn back the hands of time or figure out some way to make this nightmare go away. She loves her family and she didn't mean to hurt them in any way. She also wondered why Ralph deserted her and left her alone to deal with this problem they both had an equal part in creating.

At about 7:30 in the evening of April 22, 1954 Fred hadn't made it through the front door when he saw Henrietta rushing towards his yelling, "Her water just broke, go fetch Bessie and Rosetta. Back then, black children were born in the house and delivered by these two Mid-wives. They had a reputation for delivering healthy babies. Bessie told Emma Jeanne, "Just look at your beautiful little girl. You gotta give that child a pretty name. What's it gonna be. We have to first record her name and birthday in the family bible and later we'll have it properly recorded when we go to Myrtle Beach next week." Emma Jeanne told Bessie that she gave her baby a biblical name, Ruth who was a strong and amazing woman. She gave her the middle name Anne because that is the first name of her 7th grade teacher, Mrs. Anne Grant. Mrs. Grant always encouraged her and told her she was smart and had a lot of potential. So, she named Ruth Ann after people she admired.

After having the baby, Emma Jeanne was closely supervised by both her parents and the elder women in the church. They were about the business of helping her find a decent man who would make a good husband for her. They believed that they were helping her correct her sinful ways.

Emma Jeanne didn't like the pressure of living with a child out of wedlock and she still angry with Ralph for not marrying. He didn't deny his role in this situation; he just left her to deal with it alone. Her main complaint was he never gave her any type of support. She wasn't looking for money. Just a little bit of emotional support would have made her feel better. She thought he was being very selfish. He was thinking more about himself, his baseball career and his family.

Ralph was really afraid because things were not going the way he wanted them to go. He felt bad after losing the scholarship to college. Now, he feared that Emma Jeanne and the baby would end his chances to become a successful baseball star. Emma Jeanne on the other hand, was beginning to think she was all alone in this situation until The Itty-Bitty Committee which is made up of three elderly women from her church; Mt. Shiloh Baptist Church convinced her that she had to forget Ralph and move on with her life. She wanted to have a stronger relationship with her mother during this troublesome time, but that relationship needed time to heal. She understood why her mother was angry, but at the same time she felt that she was unreasonable and too critical of her.

CHAPTER 3
RALPH'S LIFE-CHANGING EXPERIENCE

Right after graduating from high school, eighteen-year-old Ralph Cunningham's life was changing fast. His one-night stand with Emma Jeanne had gotten her pregnant. He was urged by both her family and his to make things right and marry Emma Jeanne. He felt sorry that things happened the way they did, but he also felt he couldn't let anything get in the way of him becoming a professional baseball player, so he didn't marry her. His young life was further complicated when he was drafted into the United States Army. He was not eager to serve in the military, but he knew he couldn't get around it. Furthermore, just about every able-bodied male in those three black towns had served their country. African American males serving in the United States military had become a tradition in those towns.

That night he had the sexual encounter with Emma Jeanne, he hadn't felt any guilt at all. He went home and slept like a baby. It was while serving in the military that Ralph had a chance to see how his behavior was hurting people close to him. At first, his rebellious behavior got him in trouble. Each time he got in trouble, his sergeant, James Poindexter, forced Ralph to do more push-ups or sit-ups. There were only three other soldiers in his unit who did more push-ups and sit-ups than Ralph did. He also had privileges taken away. On weekends, soldiers who did what they were asked to do correctly and without problems could go into town. Most weekends, Ralph was still on the Army base peeling potatoes or mopping the mess hall.

All those weekends alone with his sergeant were very productive. They got a chance to know each other. Ralph asked the sergeant, "Why are you so hard on me?"

Sgt. Poindexter answered, "You are treated just like any other soldier who breaks the rules. It's really very simple. Follow the rules or be willing to pay the price."

"You don't give me the least little break," Ralph responded.

Sgt. Poindexter told Ralph, "I can tell from your attitude that you were not always held accountable for your actions. You are used to having your way, and you don't take responsibility for your wrongful actions."

Ralph thought about the things the sergeant told him and eventually began a little soul searching. He wanted to confide in the sergeant that he had gotten a girl pregnant just before being drafted. He was afraid to because it would prove the sergeant right. He began to look at his life and think about the direction he was headed. He remembered the sergeant telling him, "Ralph, before you blame other people for your situation, ask yourself what role you played in these things that are happening to you."

Once Ralph looked at things carefully, he realized that he wasn't a victim, he was really a volunteer. He had blamed Emma Jeanne for getting pregnant until he saw the role he played in the situation.

It was now clear to him that his choice to have unprotected sex was to blame for the pregnancy. He also realized that getting in trouble with his sergeant was not helping him, and that was not going to change unless he followed the rules.

Two other soldiers in his barracks told Ralph that they had gone through similar problems with the sergeant. They told Ralph, "We learned some hard lessons from Sgt. Poindexter. For one thing, he's firm but fair. He doesn't get you in trouble; you get yourself in trouble."

They told Ralph about one soldier who kept up his bad behavior until he received a dishonorable discharge. Ralph certainly didn't want that because it would bring permanent shame on his family and himself. He realized that he had brought enough shame on his family. It was time to turn things around. The thought of being dishonorably discharged made Ralph cringe. That was an awakening moment for him.

Ralph decided to make a daily effort to change. His relationship with the sergeant got better right away. They became friendly enough for Ralph to share his dream of becoming a Major League Baseball player. The sergeant loved the game and would keep Ralph informed about progress black baseball players were making. Some other black baseball players, like Satchel Paige, Willie Mays, and Hank Aaron, were being drafted into the major leagues.

Ralph was able to enroll in a drafting class while stationed stateside. He really liked doing technical drawings. He received a certificate of completion before he was shipped overseas. During the year he spent in France, he wrote several letters to Emma Jeanne but never had the nerve to mail them. He kept them with the intention of one day giving them to her. In each of these letters he expressed his remorse, saying how sorrowful he was for complicating her life. He said he wanted her to know that he understood how it must have made her feel. He said he should have given her support. He returned home a changed man.

CHAPTER 4
RUTH ANN MEETS HER BIOLOGICAL DAD

April 22, 1972 was a very special day for Ruth Ann. It was her 18th birthday and she was gearing up to graduate from Hammondsville High School in less than a month. She's among the top five students in her class. She had that same beautifully carved figure like her mother and a friendly personality to match. Throughout her high school years she did volunteer work at Our Lady of Mercy Hospital on the weekends. She was also on her high school's track team. It was while working at the hospital that she decided to become a Pediatrician. She's well-adjusted and her future looks bright.

WHEN DID EMMA JEANNE AND JOE GET MARRIED?

Emma Jeanne and Joe thought long and hard before making the decision to tell Ruth Ann who her biological dad was. That Saturday was her birthday, Joe and Emma Jeanne didn't want to do anything that may upset her on her special day. So, they waited until after supper the next day. Right after dinner, while everyone was still sitting at the table Emma Jeanne and Joe got very quiet for a moment and gave their daughter a serious look. It was a look that made Ruth Ann curious. She sensed that her mother was about to tell her something serious. Finally she said it, "Ruth Ann, Joseph isn't your biological father, but he has done all the things a father does. He made sure you had food, clothing, shelter, education and a good moral compass. We took you to church so you could learn the scripture and how to live among other people. Your biological father is Ralph Cunningham. He lives just up the road about eight miles from here. We know that he's married and has a family of his own. We talked to him recently and he said you're more than welcome to visit and meet him anytime if you want to. "We want you to think about it and let us know." Emma Jeanne said with a heavy heart. Ruth Ann and her, brothers were shocked. This news was like a low blow. It took a minute to regain their composure and get back to their senses.

During the week Ruth Ann reminisced about her relationship with her family and wondered why she didn't have the slightest clue that Joe wasn't her biological father. He always showed her love even when he chastised her. As the days passed, the hurt and confusion became less and less.

Ruth Ann thought about whether or not to visit her biological dad for two whole weeks. She sought advice and counsel from her mother. She suggested that she pray and asked God for direction. After giving it some serious thought, she decided to visit Ralph. The eldest of her two brothers Joe Jr., drove her to Ralph's house. Although it was only a few miles away, the ride there seemed like an eternity to Ruth Ann. They finally reached the address written on the paper. It was in a neighborhood with red maple and Eastern redbud trees lining the streets, All the lawns were well-manicured and the mostly brick houses, like most in the South, were detached. There was a flower bed in front of the porch filled with an assortment of daffodils. As she headed up the walkway she saw brick steps and a dark grey wooden porch. There were three feet deck rail planters hanging from the porch rails. They were spaced about three feet apart, each filled with a colorful bouquet of flowers. On the right side of the porch, there was a swing big enough to seat three adults, and on the left side, there were three slate grey Adirondack chairs.

Joe Jr., waited patiently in the car, looking everything over while his sister went to see Ralph. Ruth Ann took a deep breath and nervously rang the bell. She was about to ring the bell again when suddenly this tall handsome man appeared. "Hello, can I help you?" Ralph asked. With a little nervousness in her voice she said, ". Hi my name is Ruth Ann," I am your daughter and I just wanted to meet you." In the background you can hear his wife Sarah ask, "Who is it dear?" Ralph replied, "It's for me honey." He invited Ruth Ann to take a seat anywhere on the front porch. She chose to sit in the swing. Then, Ralph said, "Excuse me I'll be back in a minute." He went back inside his house and explained to his wife, that the young lady at the door was his daughter he told her about before they got married. He explained to Sarah that this was the first time he'd seen his daughter and wanted to talk to her before introducing her to the rest of the family. Sarah agreed and said, "Okay."

On his way back to see Ruth Ann, he went into their bedroom closet, lifted a small plank from the floor and took out a package that he had been saving for years. He kept it there just in case he ever got this chance to meet his daughter. He took the package with him as he returned to the porch. He went over and sat on the swing next to Ruth Ann and told her, "I don't know how you feel about me, but I didn't marry your mother because I felt I was too young and I just wasn't ready. That didn't mean that I didn't love your mother. I did love her and I always loved you as well, Ruth Ann. There isn't a day that hasn't went by that I was thinking about both of you." Reaching for the package he brought outside, he handed it to Ruth Ann, and said, "I've managed to save this little money for you, and I know it's not much, its only $2,000. But that's all I could to save for you. The package also contained the letters Ralph had written to Emma Jeanne, but never mailed them off to her.

Ralph told Ruth Ann, I have a wife and children and things have not always been easy for us. I've been meaning to give it to you, to help if you decided to go to college or just to help in general. Please accept this and do with it whatever you decide and be sure to give the letters to your mom." Ruth Ann took the package and said "Thank You." "Would you like to meet the rest of my family?" Ralph asked. "Sure." Ruth Ann replied. He asked her to take the package and put it away in the car before she come inside. Ralph told her to get her brother and come inside. He introduced Ruth Ann and Joe, Jr. to his wife and their two children, Ralph Jr. thirteen years old and Amy who is eleven. Now, after a few minutes of small talk, they promised to meet again with both families.

As soon as Ruth Ann returned home from seeing Ralph, her family couldn't wait to hear what happened. Emma Jeanne looked at her daughter as she entered the door. Ruth Ann wanted to put a poker face on, but as soon as she saw her mom, she gave her a big smile. Curious mom quickly asked, "How did things go?" "It was great mom" replied Ruth Ann. Joe was standing behind Emma Jeanne as was his custom. He didn't say much until he had assessed the situation. Ruth Ann could usually read his face, but now she can't quite be sure how he felt. She told her them that it was a great visit. She told them that Ralph and Sarah suggested that it would be a good idea if both families could get together one Sunday after church. Emma Jeanne responded, "Let me talk this over with Joe and we'll let you know." Joe was a secure man in his marriage, and he'd do anything that he thought would benefit his family and make them happy.

Ruth Ann waited for the right moment to give the letters to her mom. She didn't know what was in those old letters so she gave them to Emma Jeanne when they were alone. It was a good thing she did. Later Emma Jeanne when was all alone, she read those letters and started crying. She was able to let go of any resentment she held towards Ralph. It didn't change her love for Joe; it just gave her relief to know that Ralph did care about her and what she went through. She was crying tears of joy.

During the next few weeks, Ruth Ann she still had some mixed emotions. Ralph seems like such a genuinely good man, but she was taught to believe Joe was her dad and she loves him. She was trying to figure out how she was going to handle things going forward. Her mother told her that from time to time these things happen. "You just take it one day at a time and let God handle. It'll all turn out fine. She knew she could always count on her mom and dad to give her words of wisdom and comfort. Her younger brothers; Joe Jr. sixteen years old, and Jessie fourteen years old looked up to her and valued her opinions. They loved there big sister dearly and that will never change. She was a great big sister. She helped them with their school work, stood up for them when they got in trouble at school, and taught them many things, including how to drive a car. She was also crazy about her brothers. They teased her about her choice of male friends.

They really had fun with her prom date, Larry Miles. He was the nerdy type and dressed like the white boys. He wore his pants tight and the legs ended an inch above his heels. Also, he wore white socks. His social skills were not so great either. He thought he could get along with people by telling them jokes that he thought were funny, but they were not. Ruth Ann had grown up to be beautiful just like her mother. She was more focused on becoming a doctor. She received a four-year fully tuition-paid scholarship to Howard University where she'll be enrolled in their Pre-Med Program.

CHAPTER 5
RUTH ANN GOES TO COLLEGE

Joe and Emma Jeanne packed all the things Ruth Ann needed into their 1972 Ford Country Squire Station Wagon and drove her to her dorm room at Howard University in Washington, D.C. It was a small efficiency apartment with a kitchen. There was a cafeteria that served three meals a day. Ruth Ann shared her dorm room with Claudia Wiggins. It was her second semester there. The living arrangements were easier for Claudia because most of life, she shared a room with her older sister, Lola. Ruth Ann was not exactly an introvert; she was just a little less outgoing than Claudia. They became friends and gave each other support.

Neither of the girls had time for dating. They were both there on scholarships and wanted to stay focused so they wouldn't lose their scholarships. However, during the end of her first semester Ruth Ann met a young man at a campus party named Justin Booker. Everyone around campus knew him as JB. He drove a new 1972 blue, convertible Pontiac GTO, wore expensive jewelry and had his own apartment right near the campus.

Ruth Ann began spending more time with JB and less time studying. Claudia became concerned because her friend seemed to have lost focus and her grades were dropping fast. As soon as Claudia learned who Ruth Ann was dating, she was very upset. Ruth Ann was always coming in late. She waited up for her one night and gave her some background information on JB. She told her that JB was the reason her last roommate didn't make it. She told her that JB was not a student there. He sold drugs to students and some staff members on campus. She told Ruth Ann "Stay away from him because he's really a loser."

Claudia explained that her last roommate Sharon Tibbs was expelled because she was caught carrying drugs that she said belonged to JB. He denied having anything to do with drugs. The cops said it was a case of his word against hers and let him go. Sharon also got a year's probation. Ruth Ann Thanked Claudia and broke up with JB the next day. He demanded an explanation. She just kept insisting that she didn't have time for a relationship. He asked her if anyone said anything negative about him. She said, "I know about your past." Is that why you want to break up with me?" JB asked. "That's part of it." She responded. JB gave Ruth Ann an evil, hard look and said "Fuck you bitch," before speeding away.

Ruth Ann learned that breaking off that relationship with JB was not an easy task. After the break up, he stalked her on campus for weeks. This made her nervous, but at least she was getting back on track with her school work. She made it through the second semester with her grades back where they should be. During the summer of 1973 JB was arrested for selling drugs to an undercover agent on campus.

Ruth Ann was lucky that Claudia gave her JB's background. She could have gotten into big trouble while fooling with this guy. He was also a pimp. Sharon didn't tell Claudia or anyone else about the time JB told her he was running low on cash. So, he demanded that she go out and sell her body to five men and collect $100 from each of them. When she came back, she only had $400. JB asked her, "Where's the rest of the fucking money." Sharon told him "The last guy ran out without paying." "Bitch you lying." "No I'm not. I swear JB." JB slapped her hard across her face and said "Bitch you better not ever lie to me." "I'm not lying JB." She said between bleeding lips. JB grabbed Sharon and French kissed her. She reciprocated while moaning in a low voice "I love you JB. He spun her around very quickly and pulled up her dress, pulled down her panties and bent her body over the kitchen table and forced his penis into her vagina. He began pumping his fun stick faster and faster into her tight, wet tunnel of pleasure. He started slapping her big butt cheeks and asking her the same question over and over, "Who's yo daddy? Who's yo daddy?" Sharon said in a loud sexy voice, "You are big daddy." It was a good thing JB got arrested and locked up for good because Sharon may have gotten back together with JB. Ruth Ann escaped that horrible experience JB put Sharon through.

Ruth Ann began having quick flashbacks about her upbringing in the town of Hammondsville, S.C. She appreciated Ralph telling her that he always loved her and never forgot her. She also appreciated the money as his way of making restitution to her. Although she received a scholarship for the Pre-Med Program at Howard University, the money he gave comes in handy, because she still had to buy books, clothes, and many other extras that was not included in the scholarship. The anger that had swelled up inside in of her was gone. She credited her mother for taking the time to explain her situation. Emma Jeanne made her realize how blessed she was to have so many people in her life who really loved and supported her. She cherished the relationship she had with her mom and dad. They reminded her to be grateful that both men in her life are kind, thoughtful, and considerate. It could have been different. So, it didn't take long for her to think of her situation in a positive light and move her life forward.

CHAPTER 6
WHO WAS CLAIRE HAMMONDS-SHIPMAN?

Ralph later married a woman named Sarah. Sarah's mom, Claire Hammonds-Shipman, was raped at age seventeen by a white man from the neighboring town of Remington. She had just participated in a school play, *The Stray Bird's Final Chirp*. It was a story about the deadly journey of a little bird that strayed from its flock. She was the main character, a bird called Chirpy. After the play ended, Claire and other members of the cast met in front of the school teased each other about some errors they had made while acting, had a few laughs, and headed their separate ways toward home. Claire was offered a ride home, but since it was a nice warm night out and she only lived about two city blocks away so, she decided to walk home alone.

Although she knew that it was safer to travel with her friends, she was adamant and walked home alone. She made it to within a block of her home when suddenly a white man in a black Chevy Bel Air pulled up beside her. He pointed a pistol at her and told her, "Get in the car or I'll shoot you."

Claire didn't know what to do. She had only a split second to make a decision. She had seen this man from a distance delivering ice to the grocery stores around town. She didn't know his name, but she knew that face. Now he was a few feet from her with a frightening, stone-cold look on his face. He had a gun in his hand pointing directly at her head. She knew he was not going to take no for an answer, so she got into the front passenger side of the car.

"Put your head down," the man demanded. Claire was afraid for her life, so she complied. He drove to a wooded area about a mile outside of town and told her, "Take off them clothes and get into the back seat."

Sarah started crying and pleaded, "Please don't hurt me."

"Shut up and lie down or I'll kill you."

She was consumed with fear, so she lay there hoping he wouldn't make good on his threats to kill her. After raping her, she thought he was going to kill her.

Claire pleaded, "Please don't kill me. I promise I won't tell anyone."

The man gave her a stern look and said, "If you tell anybody about this, I'll find you and kill you, you hear?"

"I promise I won't tell," she said.

As he was about to drive away, she begged him to take her back where he found her. Reluctantly, he dropped her off a couple blocks from her house. "You better not tell anybody or I'll come get you."

Meanwhile, Claire's family was worried sick about her. They called her friend and were told she had chosen to walk home by herself. When Claire finally got home an hour later than expected, she told her parents that the man who delivered ice to the local grocery stores had raped her. Her parents knew who it was. His name was James Lofton. They passed the information on to the "Jarheads." They were a group of black former military men, mostly Marines, who served as community protectors. They promised the family that they would find Mr. Lofton. Mr. Lofton went missing, and no one ever saw him again. The Jarheads usually dumped their victims' bodies in the swampy river filled with alligators and water moccasins. Lofton disappeared for good, but things don't end there.

THE INNOCENT LIFE OF CLAIRE HAMMONDS CHANGED FOREVER

Claire became pregnant as a result of being raped by the ice delivery man. Her church wouldn't tolerate her having an abortion even after being brutally raped. She had a beautiful baby girl and named her Sarah. A year passed and Claire met a handsome young man named David Shipman at the skating rink. They began seeing each other and eventually began courting. This relationship led to marriage between Claire Hammonds and David Shipman.

CHAPTER 7
SARAH'S JOURNEY TO WOMANHOOD

As years passed and Claire became happily married with three children, the rape incident still affected Claire's perception about men. That mistrust revealed itself as Sarah became a young woman. She was very pretty with a knock-out figure to match. Claire always kept a distance between Sarah and her stepdad, David Shipman. Although he was the only man Sarah called dad, they never really had that father/daughter relationship.

Sarah, like Emma Jeanne, was the eldest of three children, and like Emma Jeanne, she grew up learning and accepting her moral values from her parents. She belonged to the African Methodist Episcopal Zion Church and attended Amos Hammonds' Elementary and Steve Hammonds' High School, located in the northeast section of Hammondsville. Her life was not any different from those of any other kids in those black communities. Church and school activities were a great opportunity for Sarah and her siblings to become socially competent. They got along well with their peers and adults.

Sarah, like all kids in Hammondsville, was expected to be a high achiever in school. She was an A student both in elementary and high school. She loved school, especially the extracurricular activities. She sang in the church choir and acted in school plays. When it came to taking on challenges, she always seemed confident that she could handle things. Although she was very light-skinned with long, wavy, black hair, she never acted any different from people darker than she was. She always considered herself just a part of that community. Her whole family was darker than she was, but it didn't cause any conflict in the family. Sarah loved her family. Her mother owned a beauty salon, and she'd ask Sarah to help her some weekends while she was still in high school. Sarah loved styling hair and the compliments she got from clients.

Sarah never knew her real father, but she did have a somewhat distant relationship with her stepdad, and although it was a little confusing at times, it didn't really bother her at the time. She met Ralph shortly after he came home from the military. They had a long three year courtship because he was working as a draftsman and playing minor league baseball whenever possible. Sarah on the other hand, was finishing up her degree in nursing. When they finally, got married, he slowly became the father figure that she had missed during her childhood.

Claire was a little strict with Sarah. She knew guys would be physically attracted to her, and she didn't want her daughter having babies out of wedlock. That was a concern of every mother in town, but it was especially important to Claire because Sarah was very pretty and too friendly with guys. Sarah did manage to have two close male friends during her high school years. She was never intimate with either of them. The only thing they got was hugs and a kiss on the cheek. She didn't become intimate with a man until she got married to Ralph. He was the first man she ever felt really close to.

CHAPTER 8
TIMELESS ADVICE FOR MARRIED COUPLES FROM REV. FITZGERALD

After performing Sarah and Ralph's wedding ceremony, Rev. Fitzgerald passed on some timeless advice from Jane Hells (1886) to make a marriage last forever: "Let your love be stronger than anger or hate. Learn the wisdom of compromise, for it is better to bend than break. Believe the best rather than the worst, for people have a way of living up or down to your opinion of them. Remember that true friendship is the basis for all relationships. The person you choose to marry is deserving of the courtesy and kindness you bestow on friends."

He advised Sarah and Ralph to hand this wisdom on to their children. "For the more things change," he said, "The more things stay the same."

Before Emma Jeanne met Joe, she confided in one of her friends from church that she wanted to marry Ralph so they could be a family. Her friend from gave her this advice: "It's never a good idea to go back to people that keep hurting you. They were removed for a reason. Yes, they keep knocking on your door, but you don't have to open it. Every time you do, they repeat the same cycle and you stay stuck. You deserve to be treated with respect. Sure, no one is perfect, but people who hurt your heart too much never give it a chance to heal. It's finally time to let go of people and things that don't make you feel loved, happy, and whole. Trust me, I know because I went through the same thing. It was a hard lesson to learn, but I learned that you can't start the next chapter if you keep reading the last one."

Emma Jeanne's best friend Mary offered her advice. She told her to "Think of Ralph as a door; "if the door doesn't open, then it's not your door." She also reminded her that Rev. Fitzgerald taught them that "You can't change the way people feel about you, so don't try." She went on to say, "Just live your life, be happy and forget him. That's what we do."

Emma Jeanne learned some powerful lessons from having a child out of wedlock. She learned that no matter how many things she did right in her short life, it was the one thing she did wrong that people focused on and judged her by. She also learned that sometimes the bad things that happen in our lives that put us directly on the path to the best things that will happen to us.

CHAPTER 9
HOW EMMA JEANNE AND JOE MET

Emma Jeanne needed to get Joe's attention. Her advisors were "The older women" in church called the Itty-Bitty Committee. These women, Fanny Lou Harris, Mildred Whitfield, and Maxine Yates gave Emma Jeanne explicit instructions about how to make Joe her husband. They advised Emma Jeanne to sit next to Joe and formally introduce herself, so she did. She was then instructed to clap her hands to the upbeat tempo of the hymn. While clapping her hands and moving her body, she was told to make it appear that raising her skirt two inches above her knees was an accident. She did exactly as she was instructed, and it got Joseph's attention.

"Oh, wow!" Joe thought to himself as he looked at Emma Jeanne's thighs. He really liked what he saw, and he wanted to see more. His imagination went a little wild. He wanted to know what the rest of her looked like under that beautiful long pleated dress. He couldn't stop thinking about her.

The older women advised Emma Jeanne to continue this behavior, clapping her hands and feeling the spirit. She did exactly as she was told, and it caught Joe's full attention. Joe's eyes stretched wide as he gazed upon her beautiful, plump, soft, caramel-colored thighs. He was mesmerized by her beauty. She followed the instructions and gave Joe an innocent look while quickly pulling her dress back down.

The next Sunday, Emma Jeanne followed the instructions of the Itty-Bitty Committee to sit with them while holding her baby on her lap. Joe couldn't help noticing her holding a baby and thought, "Wow! She has a baby. I think I could be a good stepfather."

The following Sunday the church, choir began singing those fast tempo, upbeat hymns. Those songs made members feel good. It made them want to and clap their hands and stomp their feet. When they started singing, everyone in the church clapped their hands. Some members felt so good, they did a little shout. You wouldn't do this in the white churches. Their church services were more subdued and controlled. It is widely believed that shouting in church is a spillover from black people's West African worshiping roots. When members started shouting, it is said that the Spirit of God hit them and they were feeling the Holy Ghost.

Following the church service, Joe went to Emma Jeanne's house and knocked on the door. Fred answered. "Well hello, Joe. What brings you this way?"

"Hello, Mr. Jones," Joe replied.

"Come on in," Fred said, motioning him to come forward. "How can I help you?"

"I want to know if your daughter, Emma Jeanne, and I could start taking company."

In the 1950s, visiting a girl and wanting to make her your girlfriend was the first step in a relationship. It was called "Taking Company."

"C'mon in and have a seat over there," Fred said, directing Joe to the large living room sofa.

Before giving their permission to allow Joe and their daughter to start taking company, Fred and Henrietta wanted to know a little more about him and what kind of person he really was. This time, they wanted to help their daughter make a good decision about the man she would bring into her life and get involved with.

Once Joe entered the house, Fred introduced him to Henrietta, who was sitting in the middle if the sofa.

"Hello, Mrs. Jones," Joe replied. Then he turned to say hello to his love interest, Emma Jeanne.

She gave him a big, welcoming smile and said, "Hi, Joe. You enjoyed church today?"

"Yes, I really did," said Joe, as he kept his focus on this beautiful woman. Things were a little awkward because each of them were fishing for the right words to say and make pleasant conversation. He didn't like having her mother sitting between them. He wanted to sit next to Emma Jeanne like they did in church. He also wanted some alone time with her, but her family wasn't having that because it was too early in the relationship. So Henrietta sat between them as they talked to each other. Fred sat across from them in his big easy chair. He kept a steady eye on Joe. He felt it was his duty to get to know who Joe really was, and he wanted to protect his daughter from another mistake.

The conversation was going well. Joe seemed like a good man, so the family insisted he stay and have supper with them. They told him that Emma Jeanne had prepared most of the food.

Joe thought to himself, "Wow, this will give me a chance to complement her." So he said yes immediately. He was also attracted by the smell of soul food that wafted through the air of the house.

He finally got his chance to sit next to his love interest at the dinner table. This was the kind of Sunday dinner that was prepared for company. "Did they know I was coming?" Joe asked himself as he sat there feasting on golden-brown fried chicken, collard greens, and macaroni and cheese. The special treat was the peach pie and homemade vanilla ice cream they had for dessert. They were not going to let Joe get too comfortable on his first visit, and he didn't want to take advantage of their indulgence, so at 6 p.m. it was time for him to leave.

The beginning stage of the relationship is called "the period of adjustment" or "the kabuki dance." The kabuki dance is similar to a king cobra's mating dance. They are feeling each other out to determine what roles each will play in the relationship and what the ground rules are going to be.

Although their thoughts and feelings weren't always verbalized, the unspoken impression given by the Jones family was that Emma Jeanne was a respectable person. Although she'd had a child out of wedlock, she still had a good moral compass, good character, and a good family who supported her. Joe was feeling his way through the family as well. After a few more visits, Joe and Emma Jeanne felt more comfortable with each other and were ready for the next stage in the relationship.

During this time, Joe and Emma Jeanne continued having a normal relationship and getting to know one another by going to the drive-in, dances, church, and other social events together. They also spent time with each other's families, and they got to know each other's likes and dislikes.

CHAPTER 10
FANNY LOU'S SOLUTION

Time seemed to be moving by very fast, and Ruth Ann was growing. Joe and Emma Jeanne had been courting for over a year, and Emma Jeanne wondered when Joe would ask her to marry him. Emma Jeanne wanted to be married before Ruth Ann knew Joe was not her biological dad. She went to a member of the Itty-Bitty Committee, Ms. Fanny Lou, for advice on how to bring Joe and her together in marriage.

Fanny Lou was a small and very fair-skinned woman in her mid-sixties. One could tell by the wrinkles on her face that she was in her senior years, but her youthful body looked like that of a thirty-five-year-old woman. She practiced her own form of voodoo. Many people in the town thought she was clairvoyant because she had accurately predicted the deaths of several people. It was also widely believed that she could cast magic spells on people and make them do things they had no intention of doing. Many of her clients were women who wanted to find a husband.

Emma Jeanne believed that Fanny Lou could help Joe make up his mind and marry her. One Sunday after church, Fanny Lou showed up at the Jones' house. It just so happened, that Joe showed up a few minutes later. He was visiting the Jones pretty regularly now. He and Emma Jeanne have been courting (Dating) long enough for him to earn the family's trust. Emma Jeanne has fallen in love with Joe and was hoping to draw him in. She shared her feelings about Joe with Fanny Lou. Fanny Lou conjured up a plan that was sure to make Emma Jeanne a magnet and reel Joe in.

As soon as Joe entered the house, Fanny Lou took his hat and jacket. She went into the next room and hung the jacket up in the closet. Then she took a fresh egg and rubbed it around the inside rim of Joe's hat. She wanted to get as much of Joe's sweat on the egg as possible. Afterwards, she put the egg away and went back into the living room and joined in on the conversation with Joe and her family. The more the family got to know Joe, the more they liked him.

Joe was so excited that they could finally go on dates. He didn't hesitate. He asked her out to see the movie The Hitch-Hiker, which was playing that weekend. This was his first date with Emma Jeanne, and Joe didn't want to ruin things by moving too fast. However, while watching the movie, he put his arm over her shoulder and occasionally let his hand "accidently" drop on her plump and fully developed breast. Emma Jeanne didn't make a fuss about that. She did make a little twisting move each time his hand touched her breast, indicating for him to stop.

Things started to get a little serious when he tried to put his hand up her dress. In a loud voice she said, "Stop, don't do that". Then she smacked his hand. She held her legs together very tight. She was more concerned that Joe may find out that she was wearing Granny panties. Those are panties that came almost all the way down to the knees. Girls were forced to wear those type panties if they had a child out of wedlock. This would make too embarrassed to allow a guy to see them wearing those old lady panties. They both laughed and whispered to each other during the movie.

When the movie was over, Emma Jeanne suggested they take some pictures in the photo booth located in the lobby of the theater. Fanny Lou told Emma Jeanne that she needed a photograph of Joe and her together. The black and white pictures, with a jukebox as the backdrop, came out very clear.

Emma Jeanne showed Fanny Lou the pictures. Fanny Lou selected one and gave Emma Jeanne instructions that had to be followed exactly. Fanny Lou told her she had to go out to the back of the house and hide behind the barn, making sure no one was present. She told her to put the photograph on a flat area of the ground and carefully place the egg with Joe's sweat on top of the picture. She then reached into a little black pouch and pulled out two red cardinal feathers and handed them to Emma Jeanne. She told Emma Jeanne she had to take off her panties, squat down directly over the feathers, the egg that had Joe's sweat on it, and the photograph and urinate on them. Fanny Lou told her that the more urine she got on the picture and the egg, the greater her chances of winning Joe's heart. The final step was to bury the egg and photograph together. The photograph must face upward on top of the egg. She told Emma Jeanne to stick the feathers on top, in an upward position, after everything was buried. Emma Jeanne did exactly as Fanny Lou instructed. According to Fanny Lou, this special" love spell" would make them fall madly in love with each other forever.

As Emma Jeanne and Joe continued courting, their passion and emotional attachment to each other grew stronger and stronger. One Saturday afternoon while they were walking through the park downtown, two little red cardinal birds flew very close to them. The birds circled them twice and then flew away. The couple could not help noticing these beautiful birds. They were surprised and delighted. They looked at each other and started laughing. Joe remembered having a dream the night before. In his dream, he saw two small red cardinals flying in a circle around a black angel. The black angel kept telling him in a low, soft voice, "Marry the woman you love."

When Joe returned home that Saturday evening, he told his sister, Ella Mae, about his dream and their encounter with the red cardinals. She told Joe, "Red cardinals are symbols of love and monogamy. They are also known to be matchmakers. If you see one when you are with someone you love, that's probably your marriage mate."

After church the next day, Joe took Emma Jeanne to the same place in the park. She was a little puzzled because she didn't know what he had in mind. Once there, he dropped to one knee and asked Emma Jeanne to marry him. She said yes! He put a beautiful two-carat diamond ring on her finger. Joe still had one more step to take before the coast was clear. He had to do the respectful thing and ask her father for his consent. They went back to her house. Joe stood in front of her dad and told him, "Mr. Jones, I'd like to ask you for your daughter's hand in marriage."

Fred put a big smile on his face and said, "Yes, Joe. I think you two will make good marriage partners."

Joe and Emma Jeanne had been nervous about what her father's answer would be. They were relieved and happy now that he gave them his blessings.

The day finally came—Saturday, June 4, 1955. Joe Bates and Emma Jeanne Jones had a formal and traditional wedding in the church first. Afterwards, they went outside and held each other's hand while jumping over a broom. This was in keeping with an old slave tradition called "Jumping the Broom." That's how slaves got married. Joe and Emma Jeanne liked that tradition and wanted to keep it alive. They were a happily married couple. During the next five years they had two boys from this union. Joe was a hard-working provider for his family, and he loved all his children and his wife. Emma Jeanne loved Joe also. They were truly an emotionally attached couple and their marriage was intact.

CHAPTER 11
THE GOSPEL HARMONAIRES

Joe, like most of the young men in Hammondsville, joined the Army right after high school. Upon returning home, a few of the black veterans were hired by the Hammondsville branch of United States Post Office. Joe's family owned that 40 acre farm. They produced vegetables, fruits, nuts, eggs and they raised chickens. Although they didn't earn as much for their goods as white people, they still made a profit. Therefore, he decided to help with the family farm business. After all, his two older brothers are dead and that left him to be the heir apparent to the business. Back then, they passed the business down to the male whenever possible because he carries the family name and it was believed that his military experience would make him the strongest family member to protect them and the business.

Most of Joe's uncles and cousins from his mother's and father's side of the families worked on the Bates Farm. They also had many non- family members working on the farm.

Joe stayed busy overseeing the farm. In additional to that, he formed and managed a popular gospel singing group called, *The Gospel Harmonaires*. Joe was always told he had a great baritone voice and he should share his natural gift with the world and make some money. His singing group earned extra money by visiting neighboring churches on Sundays' and singing as guest.

The group developed a large fans base in town and in the surrounding area. Joe believed they could do much better if they got the right exposure. He wanted to have their music played on the radio, but there were only a handful of radio stations that played black music back then. Those radio stations that did play black music became known as "Negro Stations." They were all owned by white people who wanted to tap into the "African-American Market" that offered various kinds of "Negro" music. Black people's music or what some called "Nigger music" wouldn't be played on many white owned radio stations. Johnny Mathis, Ray Charles and Nat King Cole were very popular with both blacks and white people, but there were white radio stations That wouldn't even play their music.

Blues legends James Guy and Buddy Gilmore were musicians for the legendary Sunrise Studios in Memphis, Tennessee. They attended one of the Annual Gospel Feast and heard The Gospel Harmonaires sing. After the concert, Buddy talked to Joe and suggested that he contact Phillip Simmons, the studio's owner and president to find out if he would hear their music. He knew if he wanted to make any money, they needed to get their songs recorded and played on the radio. He called Phillip the next day and told him about his group. Phillip invited them to come to the studio so he could see what they could do. They got into Joe's station wagon and headed Memphis. On the way, they had a flat tire in Collierville, a suburban town just a few miles east of Memphis. The police stopped and warned them that they should be gone by the time he returns. He also, said things are not good for you people around here. They hurried up and replaced the flat tire with the spare. About a half hour later, they were at the studio. They were all in awe of this beautiful place. There were other talented black singers and song writers there recording music.

Timing was on their side because many young white people were beginning to hear and love their type of secular music. The group recorded ten songs, five secular and five gospel songs. Just as they were pulling back into Hammondsville, they heard the first song they recorded playing on the radio. Robert, (Bobby) Wilson, the groups pianist and bass vocalist, almost lost control of the car. He was so shocked and filled with joy just hearing their music played on the radio. Leroy Graham, the drummer and alto singer said, "I suggest we keep our wits and not let this fame go to our heads." He was the senior member of the group and they all respected his knowledge and experience. He also said If we are not careful, we can easily turn this blessing into a curse." They all agreed and Willie Lee Brooks, (Wil) who played Bass guitar and sang tenor, led them prayer asking God for guidance.

Gospel choirs, singing groups and solo artist did well when they had their Annual Gospel Feast. Many young white people attended these concerts. At that time, gospel choirs, singing groups and solo singers competed against each other and were paid a good salary by the producers. They also received first, second and third place awards from music companies that produced and promoted music that expressed raw emotions or so called, "Soul Music". Gospel Music had its own categories. The Gospel Harmonaires has already won first place in both categories, twice during the last five years at the church festival. So, they already had gained celebrity status. The boost from radio airing gave them prominent celebrity status. Although they were celebrities they still had to work harder to keep their rank among their peers. The competition was very stiff and all groups were creative and well prepared for these events.

A big part of the each groups planning before a major performance was to look great and unique at the same time. Therefore, most of their outfits, suits, shirts, ties, shoes, had to be decided and tailor made. One thing was always consistent and that was Joe's powerful baritone voice leading the group. The harmony in each song was so sync that it just sounded like one strong voice. They spent many hours choreographing moves and it really paid off. It gave them a great stage presents. Joe and Will wrote most of their songs. They all played musical instruments which save them money. They didn't have to hire studio musicians.

The union between Joe, Emma Jeanne, and her daughter Ruth Ann turned out to be a good one. They were a happy family. However, when Joe's singing career began to grow and he was on the road a lot, it left Emma Jeanne feeling lonely. Although she trusted Joe, she wondered how much temptation he could take from women throwing themselves at him. He was really the first man she has had a real companionship relationship with. Ralph and she hadn't really had such a relationship. It had just been a one-time lustful encounter.

CHAPTER 12
WHO WERE THE ITTY-BITTY COMMITTEE MEMBERS?

The Itty-Bitty Committee consisted of three women, all in their sixties. They had been active and dedicated members of Mt. Shiloh Baptist Church for at least fifteen years. However, each of them had a not so squeaky clean past. The members included a little woman named Mildred Whitfield, who was one of the founders and its eldest member (67 years old). She and her third husband, John ("Biff") owned and operated one of the dance halls in Hammondsville called Biff's Place. It wasn't just a dance hall. Activities in their place included gambling, selling bootleg liquor (homemade corn liquor), and females offering intimate companionship to men. The rooms upstairs were rented by the hour to men who wanted private company with the women.

Things didn't always go smoothly at this dance hall. Biff ran the place with his younger brother, Joseph. He was called Peg Leg Joe because he had lost a leg while serving in the Army. They collected the money from food, beer, and liquor sales, and they also collected 10 percent of the winnings each time someone hit the number, from each poker game. They also acted as enforcers when things got out of hand.

Both of these men were big. Biff was six feet five inches tall and weighed around 235 pounds. Peg Leg Joe was six feet two inches tall and weighed about the same as Biff. Although he had a peg leg and walked with the aid of a cane, he won all of his fights. He'd poke a disgruntled man in the stomach with his walking stick and whack him across the head with it, sometimes knocking him unconscious.

Some weekends, the club got crowded and they needed more help. They hired two other big men, Joe Mack (Jo Mac) Anderson and Pete Yates, as the club's enforcers. They usually kept things under control. One night, however, things got out of control. Willie Lee Hudson had a little too much to drink and accused Biff, the card game dealer that night, of cheating him. All six players sitting at the card table tried to calm him down and assure him he hadn't been cheated. All of a sudden, he stood up and pulled a .22-caliber pistol from his waist. He threatened to kill everyone unless he got his money back. Biff reached for his own gun, a .38-caliber Smith & Wesson pistol. Willie shot Biff in the chest. Biff died a few hours later.

Mildred decided she had seen enough of that life and sold her interest in the club. She was a trained beautician, so she went to work for her childhood friend Henrietta Jones, who owned a beauty salon. She also decided to dedicate the rest of her life to helping wayward young women who were looking for solutions to life's problems and directions on how to get back on track.

Maxine Yates was also a diminutive woman and founding member of the Itty-Bitty Committee. Her job at Biff's Place was helping Mildred prepare and coordinate the food and collect 50 percent of the money from the prostitutes earnings. The night Biff was killed, Pete, Maxine's husband, followed Willie as he ran outside the club and tried to get away. Willie saw Pete following him, so as soon as he turned the corner he hid. It was after midnight and although it was a full moon out that night, it was still too dark for Pete to keep track of Willie. When Pete ran around the corner, Willie quickly stuck his right leg out and tripped him. Pete fell so hard that his gun dropped out of his hand. While he was scrambling, trying to find his gun in the dark, Willie shot him in the head. Pete died instantly. He was Maxine's third husband.

After the deaths of their husbands, Mildred and Maxine formed a deeper friendship and decided to figure out what they could do help the young women in Hammondsville.

The third member of the Itty-Bitty Committee was little Fanny Lou Harris. She fell in and out of love four times. She lived with the first two men in her life but never married them. She married the last two men, but all of her men usually left within six months. After her first husband left, she didn't know if he was alive or dead. That was the longest of her marriages, and no one expected it to last that long. Her second husband died from a heart attack. After his funeral, the pall bearers helping lower him into the grave fell in there with him. Some people ran from the grave site, thinking that Fanny Lou was putting some kind of spell out there trying to bring him back or bury them with him.

Rumors had it that Fanny Lou was too independent for her own good. She was the boss in her house. Her maiden name was Hammonds, and she was a descendant of the founders of Hammondsville. All direct descendants received a monthly stipend from Capitol Oil. Her family still maintained holdings in the oil well discovered on land that had been owned by Amos and his wife, Louise Hammonds.

All three of these women had very pretty daughters. They had all worked at Biff's Place as hookers. They'd take men upstairs, but it didn't always end up with them having sex with them. Most of the time they'd make sure the men were too drunk to do anything. When they got into the room the guys would fall asleep on the bed. The young women would undress them and put covers over them. When they woke up, they couldn't tell if they had done anything or not. The women would take the fee for their services anyway, telling themselves, "I couldn't help it that he fell asleep. He shouldn't have gone upstairs while he was too drunk to do anything."

The adult nightspots in Hammondsville were often referred to as speakeasies because they sold bootleg liquor, ran numbers and prostitutes did business there. These were all illegal activities. The sheriff, Billy Clark, was a white guy. He wouldn't go after those places unless there were big fights where someone got hurt really bad or killed. Before him, Ed Hammonds had been the first black sheriff in Hammondsville. He was a big, light-skinned man who was a direct descendant of Steve Hammonds. He wanted to feel important, so he tried to enforce the rules and go strictly by the law. There were just too many people doing little illegal things to have fun and keep food on the table and a roof over their heads. They kept him busy running all over the place. He finally got tired and resigned because he couldn't change anything.

Billy Clark, on the other hand, was more connected to the needs and vibes of the community. He would seek advice and counsel from the church pastors before making any major decisions. His wife Jolene was once a beautiful, blue eyed, blond haired, shapely woman. After having their daughters she gained a lot of weight and lost that gorgeous figure she had. Billy would stop in Biff's Place and take a black woman companion upstairs for the purpose of fornication. The women liked him because he'd give them a good-sized tip, and for some reason he didn't seem to get enough of them.

Whenever Jolene caught Billy cheating on her, she felt powerless to do anything about it. She'd cry, and say to him "Billy if you don't stop I am gonna to take the girls and go back home." Billy would always tell her "Honey I am sorry, I got a little too drunk and them girls took advantage of me. I promise it won't happen again."

A couple weeks would pass and he'd do it all over again. Jolene thought about cheating on Billy to get even. There were lots of men thought she was still attractive, but she knew how the law worked back then. If Billy caught her or even suspecting that she was cheating on him he could kill her and it would be considered justifiable homicide. His cheating made her so angry that she'd cry and say to herself "I should kill that bastard." She knew she couldn't kill him, because if she killed him for cheating on her, she'd go to jail for murder in the first degree. The law at that time was that if a woman committed adultery her husband was in his right to kill her. If she got caught cheating with a black man, they'd publicly castrate him and then, hang him. Jolene would have had a hot iron put up her vagina before being shot to death.

CHAPTER 13
INFIDELITY AMONG FRIENDS

One Sunday after service, Joe and Ralph's families had planned a cookout at Ralph's house. At this cookout the ice was already broken; they were quite familiar with each other. Ralph and Joe grilled the meats. Sarah helped Emma Jeanne make vegetables, lemonade, cakes, pies, and all the other things that they were having. Ruth Ann was responsible for getting the younger siblings (on both sides) to assist with decorations and setting up the card game table and horse shoes.

That day was a long day for Ruth Ann, but it seemed short because on that day everyone was happy and having fun. It was one of those days she never wanted to end. Ralph found himself reminiscing about how much fun it was to be with Emma Jeanne. He couldn't help from noticing her beautiful figure. Even after giving birth to three children she still looked as good as the first day he met her in high school. She still had the same beautiful curves, wide hips, and breasts that looked like two large ripened grapefruits. Although Ralph was married and his wife was gorgeous as well, she was considered a "redbone," which means she was very fair-skinned and had long, black, wavy hair. They had two children, but that hadn't affected her figure either.

Ralph's mind was fixated on Emma Jeanne. He was wondering what it would be like if he and Emma Jeanne had gotten married. He wanted to experience making love to her just one more time. The more he looked at her the more obsessed he became. As she moved around, the sun brightened her beautiful brown skin. The dress she wore just flowed with her perfectly carved body. When she walked past, her butt seemed to be calling him. The two beautifully portioned rounds looked like they were poured into those jeans. Her perfectly shaped body was so sexy. He even liked her white bobby socks and tan tennis shoes that matched her jeans. She was so beautiful, and Ralph wanted her to know what it would be like to have her again. "I need to have you, Emma Jeanne, just one more time," he thought. Emma Jeanne tried her best not to show it, but she did look at Ralph and wondered what life would've been like with him.

Ralph was tall, six foot two, with medium brown skin. There were a few grays in his wavy black hair, and he always kept a neatly shaped, thin mustache. He was a very handsome man. Furthermore, playing great baseball had made him a hero in the black community.

Emma Jeanne made efforts to avoid Ralph because of these feelings, but the magnetism between them was getting stronger and stronger. Somehow, an opportunity arose when they came together when nobody else was around. Ralph told Emma Jeanne what he was feeling. At first, Emma Jeanne gave Ralph a surprised look. She tried to hide her feelings as Ralph continued to tell her what was he was feeling. At that moment, she was feeling the same way, but she wasn't sure she wanted him to know. She decided to let him know that she was experiencing and thinking the same thoughts. They decided they were not going to let this opportunity slip away from them. They knew they had to go to a motel outside of town where they may be able to hide their identity. So, they planned a secret rendezvous the next Saturday at the Blue Duck Inn. It was just four miles away in the neighboring town of Cottonwood.

In an incredibly strange coincidence, Joe was having similar thoughts about Sarah. He had never dated a redbone before. He often wondered if being with her would be any different. Many black men desired white women back then. It could be because it was forbidden to have one. A redbone was the closest thing to a white woman. So, many black men chose them over darker-skinned black women. It also crossed Joe's mind that Ralph had seen his wife naked and had even had sexual relations with her. He was feeling a little short-changed because he had never seen Ralph's wife's naked body or had sex with her. Sarah was also thinking the same things about Joseph. Ralph has had another woman, but he was the only man she had ever known intimately. She often fantasized about other men, especially a man like Joe. He wasn't as tall as Ralph, but he had a more muscular defined figure and looked like he was still fit enough to be in the Army.

She wondered what it would be like to have a man like that. When Joe told Sarah what he was thinking she acted surprised, just like Emma Jeanne. Like Ralph and Emma Jeanne, Joe and Sarah became obsessed with each other. They agreed to secretly meet that following Saturday four miles outside of town at the Cordon Bleu Motel. It was located in the opposite direction of the hotel Ralph and Emma Jeanne had chosen, in the small town of Belleview.

While working all week, they knew exactly when and where they were going to meet. There was no more communication between them, so they told themselves their plans were set in stone. They had made arrangements to keep their children busy.

Midway through the week each of them became anxious, to the point where they didn't even want to meet any more. They all thought to themselves, "What am I doing? I'm a Christian. This is wrong." They looked at it from every angle. The last and only place to turn to was God, and they knew that wouldn't be helpful because they already knew what they were doing was wrong. Their marriages weren't perfect, but they weren't bud either. The desire to take a bite of that forbidden fruit was too great to back away now. The lust, temptation, and curiosity overpowered their rationality. They each became obsessed with what they had planned and felt compelled to do it, as if there was no turning back.

CHAPTER 14
SELF-WILL VS. GOD'S WILL— WHICH WILL THEY CHOOSE?

Each of the four individuals, Joe, Ralph, Emma Jeanne, and Sarah, told each of their spouses they would be working that day. There was no reason to mistrust each other. None of them gave any hint of what was to transpire. They each got up early Saturday morning and met at the motels as planned. By now emotions and anticipation had reached a climax. As soon as they were together in the rooms, before they could even undress, they started hugging and passionately kissing one another. Hormones were in full swing as if they were young adults again. Sarah managed to calm Joseph down for a minute, just long enough for them to undress. Once he laid eyes upon her beautiful frame and smooth skin he was ready to get it on.

As Ralph and Emma Jeanne were rushing through the lobby of the motel trying to escape from the hotel unseen, a church deaconess, Mrs. Lula Mae Johnson, spotted them and yelled, "Hello! Emma Jeanne. My God, I haven't seen you and Ralph together for a while. What brings the two of you here?"

"We had some personal things to discuss about our daughter. What brings you here?" Emma Jeanne asked.

"Some members of the church and I have a committee, and we meet here the first Saturday of every month."

Ralph stood quiet and didn't say a word. Emma Jeanne quickly ended the conversation by stating that they needed to pick up the children and that they would see her again at church. Lula Mae went back to her committee and told them what she had seen. The other women in this committee became very suspicious that there might be something going on between those two.

On the other end of town Joe and Sarah left their hotel in their separate cars without being detected. However, they were both still a little intoxicated from the few drinks they had prior to their rendezvous. While they were driving back, there was a farmer driving an old pick-up truck in the middle of the two lane narrow road. Joe tried to pass the truck. He sped up and swerved to get around the truck and his car ended up in a ditch. His face hit the steering wheel. There were no air bags during this time to protect him, so he received the full force of the accident. When he was able to lift his head, his left eye was swollen and both his top and bottom lips were bleeding from the left. Sarah ran her car into the ditch in back of Joe's car. Her head hit the top of the steering wheel causing lacerations across her forehead and was bleeding profusely. Joe managed get out and asked "Are you okay?" She replied in a very slow voice, "Yes, I am fine, just bleeding."

The farmer continued up the road until he reached the hospital, where he alerted them about the accident. He told them there were two colored folks in two cars about a mile up the road that may need medical care. The hospital sent out their ambulance and brought Joe and Sarah back to the hospital. They tended to their wounds and released them. Now, they all will have to face their churches, Ralph and

Sarah were members of Beacon Chapel Baptist Church in Bridgeport and Joe and Emma Jeanne were members of Mt. Shiloh Baptist church in Hammondsville. They all decided to seek the advisement and counseling of Rev. Fitzgerald.

CHAPTER 15
CAN REV. FITZGERALD
SAVE THESE MARRIAGES?

It was hard to keep a secret in these small towns. The word got out quickly, and those two married couples had serious explaining to do. The minister, Rev. Fitzgerald paid each married couple a visit. It was his normal practice to follow up on rumors, but he had an open mind. He knew it was not wise to draw conclusions until he talked directly to those involved.

He visited Ralph and Emma Jeanne separately. First, he visited Ralph who had moved into the baseball stadium's clubhouse. The Rev. asked him "Do you want to tell me what happened?" Ralph said "I don't mind." At first, he completely denied anything happened between Emma Jeanne and himself, but Rev. Fitzgerald had a sharp mind like a detective. He could sense when someone wasn't telling the truth and things weren't adding up. He explained to him that the truth would set him free; he went on to say that what goes on in the dark would surely come to light. The minister was able to get him to admit to the affair.

Rev. Fitzgerald's next challenge was to pay Emma Jeanne a visit. She was living in the house with the children while Joe moved in with his sister. Rev. Fitzgerald managed to get all participants to come clean and tell the truth about the affair.

Then, he asked both Ralph and Emma Jeanne to continue the counseling sessions until such time they could work on their marriages on their own. They agreed to follow his spiritual directions and were willing to work through this situation until their relationships with their spouses were intact again.

The Rev. Fitzgerald then, gave separate visits to Joe and Sarah. Sarah was living at their home. Rev. Fitzgerald repeated what he'd done with Ralph and Emma Jeanne. He explained to them that it was very important that members of the community and the church family provide accurate information before rumors spread out of hand. He asked each of them in separate settings, if they would be willing to be honest with him and tell the truth about what happened. He went on to say "Telling the truth would be the only way they could be forgiven in the eyes of God." They decided to tell the truth as well and let Rev. Fitzgerald guide them through this mess they'd made.

The cheating couples did not attend church that Sunday. Under the advisement of Rev. Fitzgerald, they stayed away from church for thirty days and gradually came back into the church family. It wasn't like they were being excommunicated or punished. This just meant that the minister was trying to give them a chance to heal a little before they ran into some church members who may not have been as gracious as he.

It was after two weeks of separation that Sarah dropped the children off at the baseball clubhouse where Ralph had taken up temporary residence. She dropped them off early so she had thirty minutes to talk to each other alone. She kissed and hugged her husband. They made small talk about the children and each other's time apart, and then she told him she was leaving to go to work. Ralph got some equipment from the dugout and started teaching the kids how to hit the ball and how to catch. Sarah sat in her car just looking at Ralph and the kids, seeing how happy they were together. She realized more than ever how much of a good man Ralph was and how lucky she was to have him. As she started to drive away she was thinking how much she missed her husband already. She decided that she needed Ralph back home so they could be a family again. She felt confident that they would stay faithful and rebuild their relationship. One of her single lady friends advised her to never leave a husband unattended too long because he might find comfort in another woman.

Later in the day Sarah finished work and went to get the kids from Ralph. But first she called Ralph over for a private conversation, telling him, "I'm tired of the separation. I want you home, and I want us to be together. No rush, but I hope you're ready to come home and move on with our marriage. I love you, the kids love you, and I know that you feel the same way about us. I'm not asking whether you're ready or not, but I want you to know that I am."

Ralph looked at his wife and said, "You know, Sarah, I have been thinking the same, but I didn't want to rush you in making a decision. I figured if you needed time then, that's what I'll give you. I would love for us to be together again. There are things we need to work on. Sometimes you make me feel like we are not husband and wife, but father and daughter. I don't like that, Sarah. What I want from you is to be my companion. I don't need any more kids. I have enough."

"It was the way we started out, Ralph," Sarah said.

"You acted like a dad, not a husband. Maybe I needed it because I did not know my real father. In a way, you were playing that role of my real dad, and I just played along even though I think it's unhealthy for us to act this way. I will to be your companion Ralph, but it'll be hard. So, we'll have to be patient. Bad habits are hard to break. But I can promise for sure that I will never cheat again. You're the only man for me, all I need, but I can't promise that I can make that change from occasionally acting out as a child instead of as your wife and companion. I will promise that I'll make a daily effort through prayer and meditation to make that change you want."

They smiled at each other and hugged and kissed. Before Sarah left Ralph asked, "When can I come home?" He didn't like sleeping alone.

"Get your things now and come home today," Sarah said. "I will go by the market and make your favorite dinner."

Ralph and Sarah decided it was time to move forward. They ate dinner, put the children to bed and went to their own room. The next morning they were happier than ever.

Although these couples cheated, they weren't without morals. They despised themselves after their indiscretions. It was when they put their egos aside that they felt like pieces of garbage. Each of them confessed to Rev. Fitzgerald that they felt this way. Betraying their spouses whom they claimed to love and care about took a toll on every part of their psyches. Cheating made them feel unclean and like they were failures. These affairs were just about sex and not about love and attachment. Therefore, it was just a hurtful mistake for all involved.

Without the help of an experienced and caring person like Rev. Fitzgerald, infidelity could have been the kiss of death for these two couples. He helped them come to their senses and realize who they wanted to be with for the rest of their lives and that the person they cheated with wasn't as perfect as they thought. This was truly a one-time slip, and it looked like they would all get back on track.

Sarah called her mother, Claire, and talked about this good news. Claire wasn't as happy as Sarah. She thought that Sarah should have followed the reverend's instructions and stayed away from Ralph a little longer. Sarah was disappointed that her mother wasn't as happy as she was. Claire gave Sarah her blessing, but advised her not to make another mistake by not following directions. Sarah thanked her mom and told her that she and Ralph had decided to make an even stronger commitment to each other. Her mom sighed in agreement and told her she only wanted the best for both of them. Sarah reassured her mom that everything would be okay.

CHAPTER 16
DID MARY WANT HER FRIEND'S MARRIAGE TO END?

As result of running into the ditch, Sarah caused considerable damage their 1965 canary yellow Buick Electra 225. It was also known as a "Deuce and a Quarter." Now, she had to carpool with co-worker friend while the car was getting repaired. Sarah chose to ride with her best friend, Mary Horton. They'd been friends since elementary school. The only problem with Mary was she could be a little nosy and try to get all up in one's personal business. One morning during their commute, they started talking about the weird outfit the guest preacher wore. This was while Ralph and Sarah were still separated. Mary asked Sarah, "Are you two getting back together?"

Sarah quickly responded, "I hope so. We are in counseling with the pastor and things are looking up. I really don't want to talk about that. Let's talk about something else."

Mary wanted to know how Sarah was going to handle this mess, so she commented, "I wouldn't take him back if he cheated on me."

Sarah responded, "I don't think you can say that unless you are in our exact same situation."

"I definitely know what I'd do," replied Mary.

"I told you I don't want to discuss this. Ralph is my husband. He's a great father to our children, and I love him dearly. That may not mean much to you, but my family means the world to me. You are forty years old, you have never been married, and you don't have any children. I would hate to see myself growing old like that. You may wind up like some of those old ladies in the church. Some of them have turned bitter. All they do is sit around and talk about how no-good men are. They're never at fault, according to them." Sarah gave a little chuckle and said, "Some of them are growing little beards, and their voices have gotten heavy. I know you are very independent, Mary, but sometimes you can be too independent for your own good. You are still a good-looking woman and you deserve a family of your own. This way, you wouldn't be so concerned about mine."

Before Mary could answer, Sarah changed the conversation. She asked Mary, "Would you mind helping me pick out my new outfit for the choir concert next month?"

"Sure," replied Mary. "Just let me know when."

"It'll be next Saturday," Sarah said.

"Okay," replied Mary.

They had reached Hammondsville Elementary School, where they were both teachers. After punching in their time cards, they went their separate ways. Mary remained on the first floor, at the front of the building, with her first-grade students. Sarah's sixth-grade class was all the way in the back of the building.

During the course of the day, Mary couldn't keep from thinking about the things Sarah had said during their commute to work. On the way home she wanted to scream in Sarah's ears that she was wrong about her. She wanted to tell her that she wasn't married because men are no good! But all of a sudden, she had she began thinking about the times she was raped by her piano teacher, Paul Watson, when she was only sixteen years old. It happened at church when there was no one else there. She had held this in and never told anyone about it, and it affected all her relationships with men. She felt like they were all the same.

Sarah received word that her car was repaired. "Thank goodness." She thought; it was the last day she had to share a ride with Mary. On the way home Mary finally felt compelled to tell Sarah about the rape. Sarah was shocked, but at the same time she thought it explained a lot of things. Many people thought Mary was a lesbian—a bull dagger is what they called them then. Sarah loved her friend and offered to help her in any way she could. She suggested that she speak to the pastor about it because Rev. Fitzgerald was a great counselor.

It took a week, but Mary did muster up enough courage to call Rev. Fitzgerald. As usual, he began their meeting with a prayer. Then he asked, "How can I help you, Mary?"

Mary became teary-eyed as she stared at Rev. Fitzgerald. He gave her a tissue and assured that whatever she told him would be kept confidential. He also told her that the information she revealed would never be used as a weapon against her. He reminded her that everyone was as sick as their secrets and that the healing process couldn't begin until you recognized you had a problem. Then you had to find a solution and work on that solution.

"You have been carrying resentment against this man for a long time," he told Mary. "Resentments are like me drinking poison and hoping you die."

Mary took a deep breath and told him the whole story in detail. She felt like she had taken a big load off her back. She felt a freedom she hadn't felt in years. After two years of counseling, Mary became engaged to one of Ralph's former teammates, Louis Mason.

Paul Watson had become the church's music director, but he had been dead two weeks by the time Mary told her story. Rev. Fitzgerald remembered visiting Paul many times before his death. He told Mary, "If it's any consolation, the last two years of his life were filled with pain and suffering. He was a diabetic, both his legs were amputated, and he had a stroke. Each time I saw him, he would ask me to pray the 'Forgiveness Prayer' with him. So that tells me that the things he'd done wrong weighed heavy on his heart. He never had the courage to face you and tell you directly that he was sorry for what he did to you, nor did he have the courage to face the consequences."

Meanwhile, Joe and Emma Jeanne were still following Rev. Fitzgerald's direction to stay apart. They longed for each other, but they did not want to rush and lose the opportunity to reconnect successfully. Joe was living at his cousin's house. After three weeks had passed and he'd only seen his wife twice, he felt as if his heart would burst. He decided he needed to be with her. They spoke on the phone often, and couldn't get Emma Jeanne off his mind.

She called him. "Joe I miss you so much. I need you home," she said.

Joe reminded her that this was what the reverend suggested.

"I know," Emma Jeanne said, "but I want you home. Under any other circumstances I could do it, but the way I am feeling now I need you to be home with me."

Joe said, "Okay then, I will come home under the condition that you are sure that you want to work on our marriage. That means we'll have to talk about what happened and clear things up once and for all. We both know it's going to be hard, but we'll pray and ask god for help. I believe God can make all things possible. "

They both agreed that their infidelity was not going to affect their marriage any longer.

CHAPTER 17
WILL HENRIETTA BE OF ANY HELP TO EMMA JEANNE?

Henrietta thought it was a good idea that Joe and Emma Jeanne got back together. In fact, she didn't' believe they should have even taken Rev. Fitzgerald's advice. She told them that whenever she and her husband had a problem, great or small, they toughed it out and fixed it. The family had grown attached to Joe. They liked the man he had become an important addition to this family. Aside from this, he was good person and always helpful. Just a few months after Emma Jeanne married Joe, Henrietta come to believe her daughter had made the right choice.

Henrietta wanted to continue doing things the family did regularly before the incident. She invited Joe, His family and several members of the church over for dinner Sunday. Everyone greeted Emma Jeanne and Joe with open arms. Emma Jeanne's dad took Joe and a couple of his male friends to the guest room to watch the baseball game while the women put the finishing touches on the dinner. Before the game between the Carolina Cardinals and the Bridgeport Cannons got started, Fred asked his friends "Who is going to win today fellows?" Joe said he thought The Cannons had betters players. So, he thought they would win. He went on to say "In their last game, Ralph played his best game this season. If he plays like that today, they'll have no problem. Another man is the group said that "These Minor league teams have been playing a lot of games lately. So, fatigue may be a factor today. They all agreed, but thought the Cannons were going to win and they did.

As the dinner came to an end, both church and family members let Joe and Emma Jeanne know how happy they were that they were able to work things out.

SUNDAY MORNING SERMON FOLLOWING THE AFFAIRS

It was the early morning service and there was a full house. Many parishioners came to hear the news about the goings-on between these families whose marriages had seemed so stable. They were curious to find out what happened. There was a different feeling in the air. No one knew what to expect from the pastor this Sunday.

The time finally came and Rev. Fitzgerald slowly walked up to the pulpit and said, "Good morning, family!"

Members responded in a rather low voice, "Good morning."

Rev. Fitzgerald said, "You can do better than that, so let's try it again. Good morning, my church family!"

This time the members responded much louder: "Good morning!"

"That's more like it," responded the pastor. "Before we hear the Word, I'd like to ask those in need of prayer to come up to the altar and receive a special prayer."

Rev. Fitzgerald did not want to single out the two couples having marital problems, so he invited everyone to come pray with him. In his prayer, Rev. Fitzgerald told his flock that "Humility doesn't mean being a doormat or that one is weak; it simply means being human. That, my friends means none of us is any better than others. Everyone commit sins; Praying and asking God for forgive is the answer."

He went on to say "If there is anyone here who has not committed a sin, please raise your hand." As the minister looked over the crowd, he saw a little girl raise her hand. He looked at her and said "Your sins will be forthcoming. Just bear with us and be patient and it will come."

The church got a laugh and went back to the seriousness of that day's subject. Both couples joined other members at the altar, where they knelt and prayed. When the prayer was over, the pastor directed everyone back to their seats.

TODAY'S WORD IS "FORGIVENESS"

Rev. Fitzgerald said, "Today's word is 'forgiveness. I am sure that by now most of you have heard about the infidelity between some of our family members. God gave each of us a desire, a mental and physical desire, for each other. That desire is called 'lust.' Uncontrolled lust can easily put one on the road to hell. When things like this happen, many of us are too quick to say, 'This could never happen to me.' In some cases those same people wind up doing something just as bad or worse. I've been in counsel with those family members involved, and I know they are experiencing a great deal of guilt and shame. Some of us would say, 'No punishment is too great for being unfaithful.' I say to them that we are in no position to judge one another. We have to let God be the judge. When I met with these individuals, each of them fell to their knees and said, 'dear God, please forgive me for I know I've sinned.' I could see the sincerity in their faces and hear the truthfulness in their voices, enough to know that they were genuinely repentant. So, my family, I've asked God to forgive them. I've forgiven them, and I've asked them to forgive themselves. Now I am asking our church family to forgive them. Once you have forgiven them, it can never be discussed again. Can I get the church to say amen?"

The church responded resoundingly, "AMEN!"

Rev. Fitzgerald made a great case for forgiveness. The couples involved were greeted by other members with sympathy instead of ridicule. The church was the place to go when things went wrong and they were just too big to handle. The pastor always preached that there was nothing too big for God to handle. Both couples promised to continue receiving counseling from Rev. Fitzgerald, and they did.

CHAPTER 18
CAN THESE MARRIAGES SURVIVE?

It had been three weeks since the sinful affairs took place. This hanky-panky stuff could have ended two very solid marriages. They had sought counseling from Rev. Fitzgerald on an individual level and as couples. They had all been open as well as honest about their feelings and assured one another that it had been just a one-time situation. However, each partner came away wondering if their spouse's sexual experience with another person would change their feelings about each other. At first, they enjoyed the experience with the other person, but that fun part quickly faded as they continued to get counseling. They came to their senses during counseling. It was while in counselling that they all learned that the keystone in a marriage is not sex. It the love and commitment they have for each other that mattered the most. It was very difficult to have an honest discussion about this sensitive subject, but they had to let their feelings be known so they could move forward in their marriages.

Rev. Fitzgerald was a man with great experience. He assured them that he had an open mind and that whatever they discussed would be treated confidentially, and at no point would it ever be brought up and used against them. He gave each couple a little information about a situation that had occurred in his life, and it made them feel that he was a man they could trust. That's when they felt comfortable discussing their feelings of insecurity after their affair.

While in the military Joe was stationed in Germany for one full year. During that time he had visited many brothels. Those women didn't care if you were black or white; all they wanted was your money. In the process of visiting these women, Joe had learned many different techniques about how to please a woman. Emma Jeanne was already familiar with the things Joe knew. It was Sarah who got introduced to a little different - and what she considered wonderful—experience. Joe was more patient with her than Ralph. As long as Ralph was pleased during sexual intercourse he didn't seem to care if Sarah was pleased or not. To him everything was great as long as he was satisfied.

Now, after two months of moving forward in their relationship, Emma Jeanne asked Joe how he really felt about Sarah and what they had done.

Joe responded: "Baby, we've discussed this over and over, and if I tell you once more it'll be the same. I have asked you the same question concerning Ralph, but I don't want to ask again because we both have decided that what happened that night is over and done with. There is no need to keep bringing up old stuff. You are the love of my life and nothing will ever change that, so if you feel the way I do and want to move forward in this marriage we are going to have to forget about what happened between you and Ralph and Sarah and me. If you can't let this go right now, decisions will be made whether to continue counseling or whether ultimately we may have to dissolve our marriage. I don't want to, but if you keep bringing this affair up that's where we are headed."

Those words comforted Emma Jeanne and set her mind at ease. She continued to do small extra things for Joe to try and let him know that he was the only man for her.

RALPH AND SARAH—THE READJUSTMENT

Ralph and Sarah on the other hand, were having a tough time readjusting to each other. Coming home from work one day, Ralph saw that Sarah had dressed nicely to impress him, but his first words were, "Who are you trying to impress, me or him?"

Sarah said, "Honey, I thought we had gotten past that one bad experience in our marriage. I've made your favorite meal, and I thought I would put on something nice just for you. I wanted to reassure you that I appreciate you and you're the only man that I desire."

Even before the affair Ralph had been insecure about Sarah, and he treated her a little rough at times. She was very pretty, and she would flirt with other men just to get attention. She knew that both black and white men were attracted to her, and sometimes it seemed that she wanted to get Ralph's attention and hear him yell or chastise her as though she was his little girl. He often told her that when she behaved that way. He didn't really like yelling at her because it made him feel like a father figure to her instead of her companion. The only father she ever knew was her stepdad, David Shipman. Her mother, Claire Shipman, had been raped by a white man from the neighboring town of Remington. When she told her family what had happened, they told the "Jarheads," a group of former Marines who served as Hammondsville protectors. They said they would take care of it. Claire identified James Lofton as the man who had raped her.

The Jarheads watched and followed James until they got him where he couldn't get away. He left a bar one night alone, and these big guys were waiting for him. Adam Beal (Big Slim), a huge black man, came face to face with James and asked him, "Do you like raping black women?"

James was caught completely by surprise because he'd done this several times before and never thought there would be any consequences. Now, all of a sudden, it looked like death was staring him in the face.

"I didn't have to rape them," he said while grabbing his crotch. "Them black girls like this."

All at once, Big Slim grabbed James by the head and snapped his neck, killing him instantly.

The Jarheads took his lifeless body, tied some cinder blocks to it, and dumped it into the "Swamp River." Lots of bodies, both black and white, had been tossed into that alligator-infested river. They tossed bodies there because the alligators would eat them, leaving no evidence. Therefore, it would be difficult to prove a person was murdered if there were no remains.

Claire didn't allow Sarah to become too close to David because she feared the two of them might do the unthinkable and become sexually intimate. David was a good Christian, but Claire wasn't taking any chances.

So in a way, Ralph and Sarah at times did seem more like father and daughter rather than husband and wife. Sarah didn't always like being treated like a child, especially in public and around the children. Sometimes, however she seemed to enjoy playing that role. Ralph, on the other hand, yelled at Sarah, and it appeared that he was subconsciously yelling at the daughter he had with Emma Jeanne. It was like he was fulfilling a psychological need to be the father to Sarah that he had wanted to be to Ruth Ann. Essentially, Sarah was acting out like a little girl so her dad could chastise her, and Ralph obliged her by yelling.

They decided to seek further counseling to see if they could get to the root of their problem and find a solution. Old habits die hard, but if this marriage was going to progress, Rev. Fitzgerald warned them, Sarah and Ralph would have to accept each other as companions rather than having a father-daughter relationship. He also told them that this kind of relationship couldn't last because women don't want sexual relations with their father. That was a big incentive for both of them to work on having a companionship type relationship. They vowed to make a daily effort to treat each other like a husband and a wife instead of the father/daughter relationship they've developed into.

CHAPTER 19
WHAT HAPPENED TO JOE'S BROTHERS?

Joe was the youngest of four children. Two older brothers, Samuel Jr. and Jonathan, and one sister, Ella Mae, along with his parents, Darlene and Samuel Sr., were sharecroppers. When the owner of the large farm where they worked died, he left a portion of the farm along with the house to Samuel Sr. Samuel planted sweet potatoes, watermelons, and other assorted vegetables on their farm. He also planted pecan trees. He bought a pick-up truck, and he would drive his truck from town to town selling his harvest in black neighborhoods. That was dangerous for Samuel, so he eventually built a store on his property. It was close to the main highway and about an eighth of a mile from a neighboring mostly white town. They didn't do very well with selling, but they managed. Samuel Sr. died in an accident in the pick-up truck. He had insurance that was meant to pay his family $2,000, but the insurance company only paid them $1,000. They claimed that there were missed payments that caused a lapse in the policy. Their mother, Darlene had all the receipts showing payment in full and on time.

The two older brothers used the money to buy farm equipment and stock the store. Now they were able to sell goods that they canned themselves and ice. Many people still had iceboxes then, which were later replaced by the modern refrigerator. An icebox was similar to a refrigerator. It was just a place to store ice and preserve food by keeping it cold. It was usually used to preserve meats. Some blacks, however, would bypass the local grocery store and travel further into the neighboring white town to buy ice from the white store owners. Samuel, Jr. asked Jasper Greene, one of the black patrons, "Why do you go into town to buy ice when you can get it right here?"

"The white man's ice is colder," responded Jasper.

The Bates brothers looked at one another, confused. They thought, "How ridiculous can he be?" They knew there was nothing they could do to change Jasper's mind. Many blacks still suffered from "post-slavery disorder," and there was never any effort made to debrief these people. In fact, there were very few mental health facilities that were geared toward helping these people.

After restocking the store and including even more home-grown vegetables, the business began to pick up. The white grocery store owners in the neighboring community were becoming jealous, so they came in the middle of the night and burned the Jones' store to the ground. These brothers were smart; they had insured the store. They used the insurance money to rebuild the store and make it better than before.

Business picked up right where it left off. Now they had some white people patronizing their store. Many whites were extremely jealous of black people, and they decided to go by this store before closing and set it on fire again. While running out of the store, Samuel Jr. got shot in the chest. He died instantly. Jonathan managed to avoid getting hit.

The next day he went back to the store to see if anything was salvageable. The KKK captured him, took him into the woods, and hung him. Hanging black business owners was common back then. It was meant to discourage blacks from owning their own businesses.

Joe's mother and sister and her husband decided not to reopen the store for a third time. Joe ended up enlisting in the military after finishing high school. He left his mother, sister, brother-in-law, nieces and nephews, and cousins to run the farm business. Although the business was good, Joe was never really crazy about farming. He, like many other young blacks in that town, wanted to make a name for himself.

JOE'S SINGING CAREER

After a career in the military he began working for the postal service. Joe decided to start his own gospel singing group. He had a beautiful voice, and he always sang in church. Everyone always complimented him for his great baritone voice. His family, as well as the church, feared that he would eventually break away from gospel music and start doing secular music. Joe never promised anyone that he wouldn't break away from the church and sing rock 'n' roll or even blues. He knew that money could not buy him the freedom or privileges that whites enjoyed in this country, but it would enable him to provide a much more comfortable lifestyle for his family and himself.

Church members always complimented Joe on the way he and his group sung at the annual gospel concert. They were just as complimentary about their outfits. Joe had worn a white suit, black shirt, and a solid white tie, along with a white hat and white patent-leather shoes. The other members of the group had worn blue suits, blue ties, white Fedora hats, and white patent leather shoes. It was amazing hearing them sing in harmony praising the Lord, and their dance moves were almost magical. Many people in the audience were infatuated with those outfits. Those were the same outfits that helped the group win the contest the previous year. The group did a lot of rehearsing to ensure that their moves and vocals were synchronized. They felt as if they knew they were winners before the judging took place. One could tell by the noise from the audience whenever they were on stage.

Two years passed and both families had survived the affairs. Their marriages appeared to be stronger than ever. However, Joe had begun to accept offers to sing secular music in nightclubs around town. His group became very popular, and people heard them aired on the radio nationally. Some white record producers from New York came to a nightclub in Hammondsville called Misty Falls. After hearing them sing, the men were so impressed they that offered him a contract right on the spot. The record producers invited the group to come to New York and sign a record deal worth a rather large sum of money for that time period. The group accepted and produced their first hit record. They became nationally known.

Joe's new fame created a little problem for Emma Jeanne. She didn't like traveling with the group because she had her own life established as a hair dresser in Hammondsville. She felt very secure that all those ladies who were yelling sweet nothings to Joe while he was singing on stage could not penetrate his mind or heart. The thing that bothered her was Joe being on the road so much. She felt great that he was fulfilling one of his dreams and she was happy for him and the group, but she'd rather have him home with her. It was beginning to wear on their marriage. Each of their three children was now married themselves. They all called Emma Jeanne on a daily basis to draw on her experience and ask for advice on just about everything. That was not enough, because she was missing Joe. They talked daily while he was on the road, but their beautiful house seemed more like a home when Joe was there. In his absence, things just seemed out of place. As soon as he left, she'd miss him.

They did what all successful married couples did, they compromised. He cut back the number of concerts he'd do each month and she would travel with him a little more. That worked out well.

CHAPTER 20
THE HAMMONDSVILLE FESTIVAL—
YEAR 2021

It's 2021. Hammondsville has survived and continues to thrive. It has gained the status of a small city, with some of the nation's best schools, including junior and senior colleges. There is a central city government, lots of high-rise buildings, and all the amenities of a modern city. Lots of rich white investors saw opportunities to make money, so they bought up land and helped create a downtown area with bowling alleys, billiard parlors, shopping malls, coffee houses, fast food and fine dining restaurants, cinemas, parking garages, one large outdoor and one large indoor sports stadium, museums, four hospitals, and a modern police department.

The city is now made up of 36 percent African Americans, 31 percent white Americans, 22 percent Hispanic Americans, 9 percent Asian Americans, and 2 percent other. Blacks and whites have about the same financial and economic interests in Hammondsville.

The gospel festival has survived and is still going strong. At the 2021 festival, Hammondsville has its Centennial Celebration at the Hammondsville indoor stadium. The year 1921 was when the Hammonds Plantation became the town of Hammondsville. Now it has become a small, beautiful city. The speakers at this event include the governor, the mayor, the president of the city council, and three of the oldest remaining descendants of the Hammonds family. Joe's singing group sings some gospel and rock 'n' roll.

The families have come full circle. Emma Jeanne and Joe are so proud of their children and what they have become. Ralph and Sarah have made the necessary adjustments to enable their marriage to withstand the tests of time.

CHAPTER 21
JOSEPH BATES III HAS A DILEMMA

Joe and Emma Jeanne as well as Ralph and Sarah were in their senior years. Their children and grandchildren were all grown up. The oldest great-grandson, Joseph III, turned out to be very dark, darker than his dad. Although he graduated from college and received a master's in engineering, he experienced racism based on his dark skin throughout his life. And now other young men were being promoted while he was left behind. Joe hated that. He also hated the fact that many of the white girls he desired wouldn't date him because he was black.

One Friday night while having a few beers at his favorite bar called the Pill Box, two well-dressed white gentleman came in and sat next to Joe, starting with small talk—the usual *hi, how are you* and *my name is*. They asked about the weather, as everyone did, because global warming had become more real than ever. Temperatures were reaching 125 degrees Fahrenheit on a regular basis. People with lighter skin, especially white individuals, were dying in record numbers due to a skin cancer called melanoma.

The conversation between Joe and his two new friends, Jack Hill and Bill Daggart, began to shift. Bill, the taller of the two men, asked Joe if he had ever wanted lighter skin. Joe looked surprised and answered quickly, "Yes." Bill explained to Joe that new procedures had been developed that could lighten skin and provide straight hair. The first was called melanin extraction, where the pigmentation was removed from the skin. The second was called gene manipulation, where the genes were altered to change hair follicles so they would produce fine hair rather than course. Joe was excited to hear this. They told him that he could sell his melanin, and because he was so dark his type of pigmentation was at a premium. It was worth $25,000. This really got Joe going, because this would give him more financial leeway to build the lifestyle he wanted and be attractive to a wider range of women. So they asked him, "What do you think? Would you like to participate?"

"Yes!" He answered quickly.

They suggested they begin tomorrow. The procedure would take only four hours.

The next morning, Bill and Jack called Joe very early, at 7 a.m. They wanted to ensure that he hadn't changed his mind. Other potential customers had changed their minds. They had to make sure this wasn't the case with Joe. They called and told him they were on the way, and Joe wanted to know if they had the money with them. He wanted money up-front.

"Half now and half later," the men said.

When they arrived at Joe's apartment, he placed the money in a drawer and left with the men. Once they reached their destination, an old warehouse disguised as a hospital, Joe demanded the rest of the money before the procedure. Bill and Jack assured Joe that he would receive his money after the procedure, which would take three hours. The complete process took four hours because it would take a full hour to recover after losing that much pigment at once.

They performed the procedure, and when Joe regained consciousness he ran to the bathroom wearing only his hospital gown, taking no time to change. He removed the gown and gazed upon his now porcelain-white skin. His hair was straighter, almost as straight as the average white person's. Bill and Jack explained that after a few haircuts it would be completely straightened for life. Joe, filled with mixed emotions, was beside himself. He got dressed, but he couldn't stay away from the mirror.

"How long will this last?" He asked.

"Forever, Joe, although it can be reversed, but it's a bit more expensive," they explained.

Joe received the remaining balance he was owed, and they drove him home. Jack and Bill gave Joe their direct contact information so he could call if there were any complications due to the transformation.

Joe wanted to see if his new look would work. Was it worth it? Could he finally have a relationship with a white woman, with professional women? During the course of the day he bought himself a special outfit. Later that evening he wore that outfit to Club 45, the most upscale nightclub in town. Joe went in and had a few beers like he had always done, but then something happened. He was attracting women, two to be exact. They were staring at him and giving him a big welcoming smile every time their eyes met.

One young lady was sitting only two seats away, and the other one was sitting directly across the bar from him. It was a hard choice to make for Joe because they were both equally attractive. He decided to invite the young woman sitting closer to him over for a drink. After a little introduction, they learned that they had some things in common. For starters, they were both engineers. This made the conversation between them fluid. Joe and this woman exchanged information and continued to see each other. At work and to his family Joe explained that his new look was a result of an extreme case of vitiligo. There was doubt because of the suddenness with which the condition had appeared, but as time passed they accepted his story about his skin, but they never understood the change in his hair.

Some of Joe's family and friends became jealous because he suddenly had lots of money and was able to date upscale white women, upscale black women as well. As jealous as they were, they often said, "I wish my skin was like yours."

Joe didn't want to reveal his secret, so he stuck to the vitiligo story and said that it was genetic. All the while his friends told him they wished they could be like him.

A whole month had passed when Bill and Jack ran into Joe at the Pill Box. They wanted to check up on him and find out how he liked his new look and see if there were any complications with his new skin.

"Now I realize that there are many privileges white people enjoy every day that blacks can't because of skin color," Joe explained.

Bill and Jack wanted to know if he had any friends or family that would like lighter skin. They offered Joe $50,000 for every referral who completed the procedure. Joe thought long and hard about this.

Joe loved money so, he thought to himself, "Why not? "I could become a millionaire." Joe recommended those whom he thought would enjoy lighter skin.

Two years passed and Joe was engaged to Sophia, the woman he met at the club. And she was pregnant. However, the next two years didn't turn out so great. The threat of Joseph getting melanoma was steadily increasing. He was developing warts, and his doctor told him that he would get skin cancer that was irreversible. He wanted to make sure that he was healthy to be there for his wife and children.

By now, Joe had come to realize that being white or fair-skinned wasn't as great as he thought it would be. There were far too many white people who still hated black people, calling them lazy and ignorant. He even heard a co-worker say "Black people were a waste of space."

"My job pays well, and they often want me to be in agreement with them when they call blacks derogatory names," Joe thought. "Although I am qualified, I have been promoted based on skin rather than ability. I've been promoted over qualified black people based on the color of my skin."

Joe was having serious thoughts about the person he'd become. He had money and white privilege. He had access to things he normally wouldn't be able to experience if he were still black. These wealthy, powerful people Joe now knew had connections to the system, connections to more money. But Joe kept asking himself, "Is it worth it?" In the beginning it seemed great. There were so many perks and advantages, but he was living and working against his own race and interests.

"I'm fully aware that black people do and have gotten melanoma, but at nowhere near the rate of more fair-skinned individuals," Joe thought. "Having melanoma was the last thing on my mind prior to this procedure. Now I have serious concerns about this because the warts are becoming more frequent."

One morning Joe saw three fresh warts on his forearm. He had them removed, and then he called his two old friends, Jack and Bill, to see if he could reverse this process and how much it would cost. They explained to Joe that this was a business. If he brought ten people to have the pigmentation removed from their skin, they could reverse the process. Otherwise, Joe would have to come up with one million dollars in cash on his own to have the pigmentation replaced in his skin. Medical treatment for the warts he was developing was already expensive.

Joe decided that he absolutely wanted to reverse this procedure. He could no longer keep the secret from his wife. She was accepting, but his job was another story.

"I'll figure that out later," he thought.

Although Joe made tons of money bringing in black people for the extraction, he still didn't have the million in cash, and he did not know ten more people who would volunteer to have the procedure done to them. He decided to drug some homeless men. He found enough homeless men and brought them to Jack and Bill to have the pigmentation extracted from their skin.

Joe had the procedure reversed. Now he had lived in both the white and black worlds. After giving up all the privileges of a white man, he had to be plain old Joe again. That was sometime a difficult task. He had to go back to being a black guy. Over time he made the adjustment and went on to accept himself as just a human being.

CHAPTER 22
THE CHURCH'S ROLE
IN THE BLACK COMMUNITY

The people of Hammondsville depended on the church for moral and spiritual guidance. However, some moral codes taught by the church were difficult to accept. From a moral standpoint, some black and some white people may have agreed on at least one of the restrictions. For example, historically the church strictly prohibited abortions. Women had no choice in the matter. Abortions were just out of the question even if the pregnancy was a result of rape or incest. According to the church, abortion was taking a human life, and it should not be left up to the women to decide. According to the sixth commandment *(Exodus 20:13)*, "Thou shalt not kill"—or as it is written in some translations of the Old Testament, "You shall not murder." According to the Bible, not all killing is murder. This commandment does not apply to animals. However, murder is the unlawful taking of a human life. At that time, having an abortion was considered murder by many people, as it still is today.

Black people in Hammondsville imposed some unspoken moral codes on themselves. For example, in black communities teaching children about sex education or birth control was frowned on. A person was expected to practice abstinence or be celibate until they got married. During that time period, many people got married while they were still in their teens. They got married whether they finished high school or not, and it was acceptable. They preferred marriage to having children out of wedlock.

If an unintentional pregnancy occurred between young unmarried people, both of their families would try to convince the young man to marry the young woman. They would tell him that marrying the girl was the best course of action because he had spoiled this young woman and tainted her for life.

If they were unsuccessful in their attempts to persuade him to do the right thing, he would become a *Persona Non Grata*. This meant that the young man would no longer be welcome in the woman or the child's life. No child support was expected from the biological father, but neither did he have visitation rights to see or spend any time with his child. His role in the child's life was nonexistent. However, the mother would still have full decision making authority about this even when the child was an adult. If she thought it would be good for the child to know their biological father, it would be up to her. Of course the child would have a say as to whether they wanted to know their real dad.

CHAPTER 23
THE HAMMONDSVILLE LEDGER

There were two major newspapers in Hammondsville, *The Hammondsville Ledger* and *The Tribune*. Both newspapers addressed the needs of the community, and their main goals were to keep the residents of Hammondsville informed and involved in community affairs. By doing so, it was believed that they could play a major role in helping residents make informed decisions that would contribute to the growth and development of the city.

Both newspapers had an integrated staff that consisted of blacks, white liberals, and Hispanics. Emma Jeanne and Joe's daughter, Thelma worked as an editor for *The Tribune*. In the beginning it was rough going for both newspapers because of racial hatred; many whites were not ready to allow blacks their right to vote. They firebombed both newspaper buildings, but that only made the staff and owners of the newspapers more determined than ever to establish the papers as a way of educating the community and keeping people informed.

These newspapers survived because they were sponsored by many well-established global companies. The main requirement to qualify for sponsorship was that the news be factual, fair, and balanced.

NEWSPAPER EDITORS, PREACHERS, AND DEACONS BECOME ARMED

Constant threats from the KKK and other hate groups led to newspaper editors, preachers, and deacons carrying concealed guns to protect themselves and their colleagues and family members. Many of the racists were determined to prevent black people from exercising their constitutional right to vote. They used verbal threats and cross burnings to keep them from away from the voting polls. When that didn't work, they would require them to take a test that was supposed to determine if they were competent enough to vote. They would go so far as to have white men holding vicious dogs on long leashes near the entrance. They stood right in the pathway to the door of the building where the voting took place.

In church as well as in school, blacks were taught that they must have courage if they wanted to survive with human dignity. One of Rev. Fitzgerald's favorite sayings was courage is not the opposite of fear, but it's the ability to walk through fear." They continued voting until laws were passed preventing anyone from threatening or hampering a citizen's right to vote. The challenge to make the voting process fair and give all eligible citizens access to the polls is an ongoing process even in this year, 2021.

CHAPTER 24
CONCLUSION

This book was written to shed light on some traditional values that are important and will never go out of style. It's a parent's responsibility to share their religious or spiritual beliefs and other values like honesty, fidelity, tolerance, patience, and respect for others, no matter their differences and help their children appreciate diversity and develop a strong solid social foundation. Children need to be taught that meaningful relationships don't usually occur overnight, hey are developed over a period of time.

Family support and family values are passed on to the next generation. They are not just passing fads, they are a very important part of our foundation and they serve as directions to a sane and happy life.

Visiting each other's homes for a great meal, talking about what's happening in each other's lives, the successes, failures, or just having someone to share a big belly laugh with and sharing love for each other is an important human value. Our parents especially want their children to grow up and become responsible and productive adults. They will always need our love, appreciation, and respect. This is just part of our culture and humanity.

"The family is the nucleus of civilization and the basic social unit of society. Today, more than half of all births to American women under 30 occur outside marriage, and the out of wedlock birth rate in the United States has passed 40 percent. The illegitimacy rate for black children is more than 70 percent."

William Bennett, a former United States secretary of education, is a Washington fellow of the Claremont Institute and the author, most recently, of *"The Book of Man: Readings on the Path to Manhood."*